JOANNE HORNIMAN has worked as a teacher of adult literacy, and has written a number of books for children and teenagers. She and her partner Tony have two grown-up sons, and live in a place they built themselves near Lismore.

Praise for Joanne Horniman's *A Charm of Powerful Trouble*
'A tight, intriguing, beautiful story.' www.theblurb.com

'Not to be missed.' Magpies

Praise for Joanne Horniman's *Secret Scribbled Notebooks*
(winner of the Queensland Premier's Award 2005)
*'A deeply satisfying novel on every level ...
a writer of rare skill and power.'* Viewpoint

*'The writing is beautiful ... brightened by shafts of humour ...
romantic and introspective.'* Magpies

*'Kate's emotions, her thoughts and her honesty are transfixing.
Horniman captures the anxiety and possibility of the cusp of
adulthood, using elegant, evocative prose.'* Weekend Australian

Little Wing

Joanne Horniman

ALLEN&UNWIN

I'd like to thank my learned friend Peter Furnell, who agreed to Be Here Now for me in the Blue Mountains and gave permission to freely use the contents of his Dharmic Diary and Postcards from the Edge. Special thanks also to Sarah Brenan, Erica Wagner and Margaret Connolly – and to my old school friend Maura Chambers.

Tony Chinnery and Jacqui Kent helped keep me cheerful.

Jimi Hendrix wrote the theme song and played the theme tune.

First published in 2006

Allen & Unwin
83 Alexander St
Crows Nest NSW 2065
Australia
Phone: (61 2) 8425 0100
Fax: (61 2) 9906 2218
Email: info@allenandunwin.com
Web: www.allenandunwin.com

National Library of Australia
Cataloguing-in-Publication entry:
Horniman, Joanne.
Little wing.
ISBN 1 74114 857 X.
I. Title.
A823.3

Cover and text design by Ellie Exarchos
Typeset in 10.5/16 Weiss by Midland Typesetters, Australia
Printed in Australia by McPherson's Printing Group

10 9 8 7 6 5 4 3 2 1

For Emily

One

1

In the room where she woke late every day, there was a stain on the ceiling where rain had once seeped through. Charlotte had painted it over white again, but the mark had bled, brown and frilled at the edges, like a fried egg.

Emily lay and stared at it for a long time before slowly rolling over to sit up on the edge of the bed. She stayed there unmoving. There was no need to dress, as she still wore the tracksuit from yesterday.

The house was silent, the only sign of life the grey cat that sprang down from the top of the piano to follow Emily into the kitchen. It arched its back hopefully in front of the refrigerator, but Emily ignored it. She let herself out of the house into the cloudy afternoon, walking through damp suburban streets till she came to the edge of town, and the lookout perched high above the valley.

In front of her there was only the sky, and the tops of the

trees. The forest floor was hidden, but the smell of it drifted up, dank and earthy.

She was usually the only person there. But today she became aware of something behind her: a dark shape like a column, and a fluttering, like wings.

It was a young man. He stepped over the fence and stood on the edge of the huge drop as if he was afraid of nothing. He wore a great black overcoat, and he raised his arms and stood with his hands clasped behind his head. His coat was too heavy to flutter out behind him, but she imagined it fluttering. She imagined wings.

He turned to look at her, and it was as if he recognised her, and had known her for a long time. He had light-coloured eyes, and pale skin. Black hair curled round his face. He stepped back over the fence and stood beside her, leaning over the railing, so close that she could smell the fresh scent of soap on his skin.

'I didn't notice you standing there at first,' he said. 'I like to look at the view without the fence between. I don't do it if there are people here.'

She said, 'It's dangerous to stand out there,' surprised that her voice worked at all. He was the first person she'd spoken to all day.

'Yes. But then, life's never totally safe, is it?' He smiled, and held out his hand. 'Anyway, I'm Martin,' he said.

'My name's Emily,' she said shyly, taking his hand briefly and keeping her eyes averted from his face.

'Do you come here often? Sorry . . . that's meant to be a pickup line, isn't it? I'm not trying to pick you up.'

Emily hadn't thought that he was. She knew she no longer looked like the kind of girl anyone would want to pick up.

'I come here every day.' She stared across the top of the trees. It was like an ocean – the endlessness and the tossing of the leaves like foamy waves. 'This is the first time I've lived away from the coast.' She heard herself saying it, as if her voice belonged to someone else.

'Do you like it here?'

'I don't like anywhere much. It's just a place to be, isn't it?'

He looked at her, but he didn't say anything, and they stood staring at the view for a bit longer. Then he said, 'I have to go now, and get my son from pre-school. Might see you again some time, Emily.'

She followed him, through instinct, or through not knowing anything better to do. When he realised what she was doing he waited for her to catch up. She listened to the sound of their footsteps through the fallen leaves, and the currawongs calling from the sky. He looked down at her and said, as though they'd been in the middle of an ordinary conversation, 'I'm one of those stay-at-home dads – my partner's the one working at the moment while I look after Pete.'

And Emily found herself saying, as if she was someone used to having such a conversation, 'Do you enjoy that?' And he replied, 'Yes . . . yes I do.'

At the pre-school, mothers gathered at the fence. Emily stood with her hands in her pockets. A child exploded through the gate, waving a painting. 'Look what I did, Dad! This is us at the beach!'

Emily stepped back as if something large and fast had roared past on a freeway. Martin held the child by the shoulder to steady him.

'I like what you've done here – all this blue.'

'They're the waves, Dad. And this is the sky. I made it purple.'

'Great colour for sky! And is this me? The tall person here?'

'Yep!'

Martin took the picture and rolled it up carefully. 'Ready to go home?'

The boy looked at Emily, and she looked away.

'Pete, this is Emily. Emily, this is Pete.'

'Hello, Emmy.'

'*Emily,*' she told him. 'My name's Emily.'

But he didn't reply. 'Let's go home, Dad,' he said, pulling Martin by the hand.

She went with them, one step behind, listening to them chatting about this and that. They halted in front of a cottage, an old timber place with ragged trees in the front yard and a broken-down verandah and peeling front door. 'This is home,' said Martin, looking at her with a smile. 'See you another time, Emily.'

Pete rushed to the front door and flung it wide, revealing a hallway. Martin switched on the hall light and they disappeared into a room at the side. The hall was bathed in a golden yellow light that made it stand out against the darkness of the winter afternoon, and Emily stood for a long time, staring at it. It looked like a place where people were happy.

Then Pete came running into the hall with his arms held

out like an aeroplane. Without noticing Emily still standing there, he zoomed around for a while until he reached the front door, and pushed it shut with a bang.

2

Emily let herself in, and heard Charlotte call out 'Hel-lo-o!' from the kitchen. She didn't reply, watching herself reflected dimly in the mirror of an old carved wardrobe that stood at the end of the hall. She looked like a stranger even to herself.

Bookshelves, stuffed full, lined the narrow passage. Charlotte's small cottage was a space that seemed to grow more constricted each day as her possessions took over. One day she and Emily would each have to hollow out a body-sized space to exist in.

Emily went through the doorway that led to the living room. A dresser filled with crockery, a sideboard and a piano stood against one wall. Three sofas faced them across the narrow room, and two coffee tables squeezed into the space in the middle. Every surface was covered by books, papers and ornaments. There were pots of ferns and African violets everywhere.

Charlotte's own paintings decorated the walls, along with prints of famous pictures. Charlotte's house was a place where lovers floated embracing in the sky, and an angel in a green dress carrying a posy of flowers flew through a window near the Eiffel Tower.

Emily went through to the kitchen, where Charlotte sat, a cup of strong tea in front of her and a welcoming smile on her face. Both Charlotte and her wood fire emanated warmth. Why then did Emily always feel so cold?

'I was thinking of making veggie pasta for dinner,' said Charlotte.

'Oh – I'll help, then.'

Emily lifted a pile of papers from the seat of a kitchen chair and hesitated, wondering where to put them. The benches were already piled high with newspapers, and books and folders. A pair of earplugs lay on top of a laptop. An electric drill sat in a bowl full of opened letters and postcards and offers from the takeaway pizza shop. She put the pile of papers on top of an already teetering pile on the bench and sat down.

Charlotte found some vegetables and a chopping board and put it all in front of Emily, with a knife. 'Your mother rang while you were out,' she said.

Emily didn't respond.

'Do you want to ring her back?'

'No.'

Charlotte looked at her searchingly. 'Okay then. Maybe another time,' she said.

Emily frowned, and placed an onion on the chopping board. She heard Charlotte let herself out the kitchen door. There was a shed in the yard where she painted pictures, and at the end of each day she kept going to look at what she'd done earlier, unable to resist another daub here and there.

Emily fingered the serrated blade of the knife. She knew

from experience that it was hopeless for chopping vegetables, but it was the one that Charlotte always gave her. The
chair made a rasping sound as she stood up suddenly. She
found herself at the drawer where Charlotte kept her knives.
She knew them all by heart: the one with the short blade for
fruit; the bread knife made of one piece of continuous metal;
the older, blunter bread knife with the wooden handle; a set
of six steak knives they never used since neither of them
liked steak; and the old Chinese cleaver with the wooden
handle polished smooth from years of use.

She took the handle of the carving knife that was kept at
the back of the bench and drew it out of its holder. The blade
was smooth and fine. She pressed the tip to a finger and a
bead of blood appeared on her skin. Quickly, knowing just
how much pressure was enough, she drew the blade across the
top of the finger. Her heart flipped over at the sting of pain;
she felt a thrill at the line of blood that welled out. She stared
at it for a moment, and then reached for a teatowel.

Charlotte came into the room.

'Oh, Emily, what on earth are you doing? That's a carving
knife for meat!'

Without a word, Emily allowed Charlotte to wash the
blood away and cover it with a bandaid.

They ate at the dining table, which Charlotte always set with
linen placemats and a small vase of flowers, a glass of wine for
herself and juice for Emily. After making an attempt to eat the

pasta, Emily excused herself and went to bed. Charlotte stayed up listening to music and poring over her books of paintings.

Emily lay very still in her narrow bed. The house had only two small bedrooms, and the spare one was now Emily's. Or so Charlotte told her. To Emily, it didn't feel like hers. It was simply a place to be.

Like the rest of the house, the room was full with the overflow of Charlotte's earlier life – a sewing machine, stacks of photo albums, and lamps with frilly shades. She'd offered to move it all out to the garage to give Emily more space, but Emily had told her not to bother.

Apart from a few clothes, the only thing Emily had brought with her to the mountains was a cloth-covered notebook patterned with blue stars, which she kept wrapped up in a tiny baby singlet in a suitcase under the bed. Most nights, unable to sleep, she took it out, held the bundle to her face for a moment, and breathed in the odour of it. She had no need to read what was written in the book. She knew very well, since she'd written it herself, at a time that seemed far away from this time and the person she was now. She put the bundle back into the suitcase and stowed it away, then lay listening to the soft music of a symphony playing in the living room. The bandaid was a little too tight on her finger, which throbbed pleasantly, like a heartbeat.

If her finger throbbed, she must be alive.

The grey cat settled down on her chest. It was a young cat, dense with muscle, and it let her know that she'd invaded its space by sleeping on top of her every night. First it trod in the one spot with its front feet, and then it turned itself round and round in a circle before it settled, purring heavily.

Now, the feeling of contact with a warm, living being made her cry, and she lay on her back in the shadowy room with tears trickling silently into the pillow. Then, because she was so exhausted, she fell asleep.

If she dreamed, it was a dream of leaving, a dream of a bus station and the interior of a darkened bus where she slept fitfully, in between the flash of lights appearing along the highway. She didn't think of what she'd left behind, and as for arrival – for Emily there was no arrival, no place where she was happy to be.

She woke with the house still and silent, her face wet with tears, and lay in the dark, crying, as she did almost every night. She huddled there, unable to move, feeling the darkness almost crushing her.

Dear You,

You are here. i don't know how i know that this is the beginning of you. i just do.

i should be afraid.

But all i feel is, we can do this. You and i.

Nobody knows about your existence yet but me. You are my secret. We'll be all right. i'll look after you, always.

11

3

Emily woke late, tipping the cat off her chest. It landed on the floor, tail flicking back and forth.

In the bath, she lay back and stared at the orange and green tiles on the wall through the mist of steam. Her hair floated out behind her. She tugged the bandaid off and squeezed until blood seeped from the cut.

Her knees were pale and sharp, her legs thin.

She squeezed a blob of shampoo onto her hand. When she rinsed her head under the tap, little islands of foam floated in the water. Her hair felt slimy to touch.

She dressed, and went into the silent kitchen. Charlotte was up already; she'd be out in the shed, with her paintings. On the kitchen table a white cereal bowl floated on pale green placemat with a spoon laid ready beside it. Emily went out to the windy garden, stopping for a moment at the door of the shed. Charlotte stood with her back to the door, at her easel.

'Emily? Emily?'

But Emily was already away, up the pebbled garden path and through the fishtail ferns that flopped damply in front of her. She went out the gate and up the road, head down, hands in pockets.

She walked down streets lined with winter trees, and reached the town centre, where rugged-up shoppers seemed to float past her. Her world was full of floating people, who parted as she approached. She avoided looking at faces, which had a habit of looming at her.

She bumped into someone. *Sorry*, she said, but only silently, to herself.

'Idiot!'

Emily flinched. It was her fault. Everything was her fault.

A fat man in a maroon windcheater walked past. 'Girls are sharks,' he said. Emily turned to watch him. 'Girls are sharks.' She walked around the block and encountered him again. 'Girls are sharks,' he repeated, casting a furious glance in her direction. 'Girls are sharks.' He made her feel that she ought not exist.

Emily walked back towards Charlotte's place and passed the house that she was sure (or almost sure) she'd seen the night before. The front door was open the way it had been last night before the little boy ran out and slammed it shut.

She went through the front gate, up the steps, and paused at the open doorway. The hall held two bicycles, one with a child's seat at the back, pairs of boots in many sizes, and a hallstand full of hats and scarves. She knocked.

No one seemed to hear, but there must have been someone home. She could hear music coming from the back of the house. She was about to turn and leave when Martin appeared from a room at the far end of the hall with a tea-towel slung over his shoulder and an egg-slice in his hand. His face had an enquiring expression. 'Hello?' he said, and she could see that he didn't recognise her. But then he smiled. 'Emily, come in!'

'We were just making pikelets,' he said, leading her into a big old kitchen at the back of the house. 'Pete – look who's here. It's Emily. You remember Emily?'

'Yep!' said Pete. He was kneeling on a chair at the kitchen table, watching a batch of pikelets in an electric frypan. 'Dad,' he said urgently. 'I think these need to be flipped over now. Can you give me a hand?'

Emily found that she was afraid of this child. He was so sure of himself. And she wasn't used to children; she had no brothers and sisters. She wanted to turn right round and walk out.

Martin smiled at her apologetically. 'Pete's too interested in the pikelets to be polite,' he said, flipping them over. 'They'll be ready in a minute, and then we can eat.'

Sitting with Martin and Pete in the warm kitchen with the radio playing soft music in the background gave Emily an appetite. She smothered several pikelets with butter and honey and ate one after another, before stopping, suddenly full, with a burp.

'Excuse me!' said Pete. He had huge dark eyes, with feathered brown eyebrows, and a way of glaring at her.

'Sorry . . .'

Martin smiled and took another pikelet.

There were photos on a pegboard on the kitchen wall. Emily looked at them surreptitiously while Martin washed the dishes and she wiped them. There was a young woman holding Pete's hand.

'That's me!' said Pete. 'With Cat.'

'Cath?' Emily wasn't sure she'd heard properly.

'No. Not Cath. Cat! Like the *animal!*' Pete yelled.

'Pete . . . shoosh . . . not so loud. You don't have to yell,' said Martin.

'She's my mum. She's at work today.'

There were other pictures. Of friends and relatives, at lunches, dinners and picnics. Of Cat holding a baby. The sight of it made Emily's skin turn cold. Pete started to explain them all, but Emily wasn't listening. She threw the teatowel onto the table and went out the back door, standing with her head pressed against the timber wall of the house. Her eyes were dry, but inside she was all turmoil.

'Are you all right?' said Martin, who had followed her out.

'Yes,' she said. 'I just remembered I have to go.' She fled down the side of the house without looking back.

When she arrived back at Charlotte's place, it smelt strongly of carrot soup. The cat was curled up on a wooden chair in the kitchen, and the old glass bottles on the window ledge were coloured bright blue, or green, or clear.

'You didn't eat any breakfast,' said Charlotte, with a frown. She had cleared everything from the cluttered table and seemed to be in the middle of a bout of house-cleaning.

'I ate something out.'

Emily felt the world loom darkly around her, as if something terrible was about to happen at any moment. She leaned against the sink and closed her eyes to make the feeling go away. She felt Charlotte gently remove a dishcloth from her hands; she'd been wringing water all over the floor.

'How about I run you a nice warm bath?' said Charlotte.

In the bathroom Emily turned on the tap to make the water even hotter and lay back and stared at the orange and green tiles through the steam. She closed her eyes. If she thought of nothing she could get through the next bit of the day before bedtime.

i've been thinking about all the things that i'll be able to show you. Like horses.

There is nothing quite like the smell of a horse. It's all hay and sunshine and sweat. A horse's skin is something else, too! There's a sort of shiver it gives sometimes, when the muscles move under the surface, that's like wind rippling the surface of water. It's just so . . . sexy somehow!

i'll be able to take you to the beach. The colour of waves is amazing — never the same two days in a row. i look for shells there — i always hope for a perfect, unblemished one. We'll start a shell collection, and i'll teach you all the names.

One day i rode a horse bareback on the beach. It was magic. Just me and the power of the horse galloping, and the smell of its sweat and the smell of the sea. i wanted to ride up the beach for ever, but i turned round and came back.

4

Emily went back to Martin's place. The front door was again open, next time she turned up. The house had polished floorboards, and bright paint on the walls. Everything was clean and bare. Charlotte's house was like a cave, but Martin's was a broad plain, full of light and air. She glanced into rooms as Martin led her through to the kitchen. The bathroom had an old claw-foot bath and worn lino. In the living room there was no proper furniture, just beds for couches, and chairs that didn't match. But they were covered with colourful throws, and the place was tidy. There were cane baskets on the floor filled with toys and children's books.

The shabby, old-fashioned kitchen reminded her of her grandfather's place. The cupboards had peeling green paint, and there was a chimney where a wood stove had once sat. A wobbly laminex table with plastic-covered chairs sat in the middle of the room.

Martin told her the house had been a deceased estate. Even in this shabby condition it had been expensive enough to buy, and it would be ages till they had the money to fix things up properly. He thought it was fine the way it was, anyway.

Pete was at pre-school that day. Martin walked about the kitchen with his bare feet poking out from the bottom of frayed jeans and a teatowel slung over his shoulder. He went out to the laundry and put on the washing, then pottered around the kitchen while she watched. He rinsed some seeds sprouting in a jar, and put some lentils to soak in a bowl.

That day, they started painting Pete's room yellow. Martin had already moved all the furniture and covered the floor with newspaper. He found a big old shirt to protect Emily's clothes, and a spare brush. She took off her shoes, and started to paint. Martin worked on one side of the room and she on the other; every so often she glanced over at him, and he smiled at her.

Because she said very little, Martin did all the talking.

He told her that he and Cat took it in turns to be the one with a full-time job, so that someone would always be there for Pete, even though he was at pre-school three days a week. Cat had been working since Pete was two – he had just turned five, and they thought he'd be ready for school next year. She was a theatre sister at the hospital; Martin was a teacher.

'But I just do a bit of relief work now and then when Pete's in pre-school. We can get by on less money.'

He went back to slapping yellow paint on the walls, and the only sound for a while was music from the radio in the kitchen.

The timber walls had gaps and Emily had to press the bristles into them to fill them with paint. Her wrists began to ache, and a blister formed on one of her fingers.

When they stopped for a cup of tea, the mist had lifted

and the back yard was filled with sunshine. Emily took off her paint-shirt, pushed up her sleeves, and sat on the back step with the sun warming her bare feet.

Martin sat on the old brick path and sipped tea. He opened a tin of tobacco and rolled a narrow cigarette, but pinched it out after a few puffs.

'Well, that's me,' he said. 'What about you?'

Emily looked up.

'You've let me do all the talking.'

'There's nothing much to tell,' she said. 'I'm staying up here with my godmother. Having a kind of holiday.'

That wasn't exactly the truth but it wasn't a lie, either.

Martin lit his cigarette again and squinted through the smoke. 'Cat hates me doing this. It's one of my bad habits. I only do it when Pete's not home.'

He stubbed out the cigarette and put it into the tin, then went inside and came out with a notebook. He scribbled something into it, paused to think, and scribbled again.

'What are you writing?'

'It's a kind of journal. It's where I hang out. I've just written: *Mist has lifted – beautiful spring day. Who is here with us: a small brown bird perching on the lemon tree. There's a trail of ants along the path. A girl with brown hair (Emily) sits on the back doorstep, a smudge of yellow paint on her foot.*

'Staying home all the time sucks something out of me. So I try to stay in touch with the world by noticing things and writing them down. I record who is here with us. Who is sharing this world. With us humans, I mean.'

Even with the sun on her head and feet, Emily felt dark and cramped. She thought that Martin had a largeness to him – a big airy space inside. His chest must never be constricted by sorrow. Inside, he was all rolling hills and gentle breezes.

They did an entire first coat of the room by the time Martin had to pick Pete up from pre-school. As Emily washed yellow paint from her hands at the garden tap, Martin said, 'Want to come for the walk?'

In the hallway, he put on a hat and coat. He looked at Emily's thin polar fleece jacket, and reached out for a long wool scarf, which he handed her. 'You need a hat,' he said. 'Pick a hat, any hat.'

Emily chose a knitted one with rainbow stripes. Martin straightened it for her, turning up the brim so he could see her face. She felt like his child; at any moment he might lean forward and pat her on the head.

He took long strides, and Emily had to hurry to keep up with him. They were late arriving at the pre-school, and almost all the children had gone. 'Dad!' called Pete, running to the fence. When he saw Emily, he stopped. 'You're wearing Cat's hat,' he said.

'Pete, it's all right,' said Martin. 'Emily didn't have a hat. I said she could wear it.'

'But Dad – she can't keep it! It's Cat's.' He shoved ahead of them and walked quickly along the footpath, so that all Emily could see was the severity of his back, with a small black backpack bouncing along on top of it.

Back at their house, Emily unwound the scarf from her neck and draped it over a peg. She removed the rainbow hat and placed it next to the scarf. She wondered if she ought to go now, but followed Martin and Pete to the yellow room where Pete was standing in the middle of the floor saying, 'Wowee! Wowee!', his hands on his hips.

'It needs another coat tomorrow,' said Martin. 'Since you'll be at home you can help if you want.'

Pete looked at Emily. 'But not her,' he said quickly. 'We can do it by ourselves.'

'Pete, that's not nice.' But Pete had already run out of the room, and Martin looked at Emily and grinned ruefully.

The days were lengthening, and it was still warm. Emily knew she should go back to Charlotte's place, but she hadn't the energy for it. Martin and Pete sat out on the grass sharing a plate of cut-up oranges; she lay under the lemon tree close by and closed her eyes. The dread that she had lived with for months settled even more insistently into her chest, so that she felt that she would soon stop breathing.

Then she noticed the sweet, sharp smell of skin, and opened her eyes. It was Pete. He stared down at her and held out a section of orange, asking if she would like some.

She didn't reply, and he pressed the wedge of fruit onto her opened mouth and squeezed. Juice ran into her mouth. She closed her eyes and swallowed, and lay there with her mouth filled by the skin of the orange.

21

'Is it nice, Emmy? Is it?'

Pete patted her face. His hand was soft. She felt she hadn't been touched tenderly like that for a long time. She kept her eyes tight shut, but tears came from under her eyelids.

And then Pete asked her why she was sad, and it seemed to her that no one had ever before noticed that simple fact, but she couldn't speak.

'Dad . . . why is she sad?'

Martin said, 'She just is, Pete. Everyone gets sad sometimes.'

And they both sat there with her for a long time, and didn't press her to say anything, and after a while she got up and said goodbye to them and left.

Today i told Matt about you. i watched him closely for his reaction, for any sign that you might not be welcome to him.

You can't count his initial hesitation. Then − Are you sure, he said.

− i'm sure.

− We'll keep it, yeah? was the first thing he said.

And then he hugged us close.

− Yeah, i said.

It was such a relief to tell someone.

Emily lay in bed and listened to the sounds of Charlotte's house. Even if Emily hadn't been there, it would still have sounded exactly the same. Sometimes she felt that she didn't exist, that she somehow filled no space in the world.

A door opened and closed with a hollow sound. The toilet flushed. There were footsteps down the hallway.

The sounds were remote and peaceful, and Emily, who had spent what felt like most of the night awake, turned over and closed her eyes again.

The cat had deserted her; it yowled in the kitchen. The refrigerator door opened and closed. A dish rattled.

She stayed in bed until well after Charlotte had gone out to her shed, and after dressing she just had to get out for a walk. She didn't enjoy walking, but it helped her not to think.

She trudged to the lookout, stayed for as long as it took to glance down into the valley, and then went back. Something took her to Martin's place.

It was a week since her last visit, and on the way up the hall Martin showed her Pete's room, where the painting had been completed. It was a bright, glorious yellow.

'It's beautiful,' she said flatly.

Emily knew that the room, so optimistically bright and still smelling of fresh paint, should be admired. But she didn't *feel* it was beautiful. Its freshness and hopefulness rather oppressed her. She lay down on Pete's bed and closed her eyes, and when she looked up, Martin was standing there with two cups in his hands. Not tea this time, but hot chocolate.

They drank it in the back yard. For a little while he allowed her to sit hunched with her hands pressing the sides of the warm cup, and he didn't try to rush in with words; he waited for her to speak, and when she didn't, he squeezed her shoulder softly and said, 'I was planning to replace some rotten boards in the bathroom. Want to help?'

They worked quietly. He asked her to hand him the tools, and got her to measure the length of the new lining boards. 'I try to get stuff done while Pete's not here,' he told her. She said nothing, just watched him. He bashed his thumb with the hammer and laughed. 'Shit!' He sang a song while he worked: 'Eagle Rock'. But without any backing music it sounded thin and wistful.

After a while she drifted away, back to Pete's room, where she lay on the bed listening to the sounds of hammering and sawing. The rhythmical sounds, and the way the timber house moved in response to the hammering, lulled her to sleep. She felt someone come into the room and drop a soft rug over her feet.

When she woke it was a different time of day, and the whole quality of the light had changed. Pete was standing next to her, saying, 'That's *my* bed, Emmy! It's mine!'

'I'm sorry.'

But he forgave her quickly.

'Draw with me, Emmy! Draw with me!' A piece of paper was thrust at her, and soon she was crouching on the floor beside him. She was astonished at how physically she felt his presence – he had a ripe, yeasty odour, and when he leaned against her he was surprisingly heavy.

He scrawled over the paper, making a random pattern, and Emily filled in the spaces that were formed with squiggles, spots and stripes of various colours.

'What are you drawing?' said Martin, coming into the room with a plate of cheese on toast, which he placed on the floor next to her.

'It's a map,' said Pete. 'A map of where you're going when you don't know where you are.'

'Write that,' he ordered Emily. So she wrote at the top: A Map Of Where You're Going When You Don't Know Where You Are.

She'd slept through lunch and was starving hungry. She crammed cheese on toast into her mouth while she wrote, and spots of grease appeared on the paper.

That night she switched on the lamp beside her bed and found a piece of paper. For a while her pen hovered and was unable to make a mark. She struggled for words. In the end she wrote:

Dear Matt,
i hope you are well. i think about Mahalia all the time. i think about both of you, and i'm so grateful that you are there for her. i know you'll be looking after her really well.

i can't come back just yet
i'm sorry
Emmy

i want everything for you. The moon and the stars and the sea and the entire universe. i want everything for me too. i want you and Matt and me 4 ever and ever.

Having you with me makes me greedy for life — more greedy even than i used to be. i want Everything. Nothing less than Everything will be enough. Not just for now, but for the whole of my life.

6

Her mother rang.

Charlotte took the call. She signalled to Emily, but Emily shook her head and went outside to get away from the conversation. It was very early spring, and the earth was still cool. Blossoms had struck out bravely, only to be withered by blasts of cold.

Two little girls played in the garden next door. They had constructed a cubby with a blanket nailed to the fence. Emily peered surreptitiously through the palings. The children had tiny plastic plates filled with grass and flowers, and small cups of water. Four dolls sat obediently in a circle. Two pairs of small human hands ministered to them. Their voices floated through the fence, piping and childish.

Then they noticed her watching them, and ran inside.

Charlotte came out and hesitated under the clothesline. 'I wish you'd spoken to her, Emily. She means well.'

But Emily had slammed out of the garden, her feet pounding along the path.

Martin took one look at her face and suggested that they go for a walk. Emily had come without dressing for the weather, so he found her a jacket. Again, she wore the wool scarf from the peg in the hall, and Cat's rainbow hat, and Pete didn't object this time. He was like a puppy, eager to be off.

In the park Pete ran around and around in circles, his feet scattering pigeons. Martin chased him, veering off at one point to run over to where Emily leaned against a tree. He tried to pull her out to join them.

'Bet you can't catch me, Emmy!' Pete yelled.

Emily's heart wasn't in it (she had no heart), and her legs were heavy and reluctant. But by the time Martin and Pete had collapsed on the ground, and Emily came panting up to them, she was surprised to find a faint purring in her chest, a few bubbles of air that made her remember what her life had once been like.

She waited on the grass while Martin and Pete went to the shop in the street opposite to buy iceblocks, and she and

Martin sat on the grass to eat theirs while Pete went off to the sandpit to play. He sang to himself, and laughed. Emily noticed how many times in a day Pete laughed – he was always finding something to delight him. Grown-up people laughed very rarely. It was a long time since Emily herself had laughed at anything at all.

'Can't you talk to me, Emily?' said Martin. 'I might be able to help.'

But she shook her head.

'Smile, then.'

Emily turned up the corners of her mouth.

When Pete ran over and said, 'Emily, what's the most delicious icecream flavour you can think of?', she replied with a show of energy, 'Vegemite! What's yours?'

'Broccoli,' he said, entering into the game. 'Guess what flavour Cat would like?'

She shrugged.

'Sardine!' he said, and ran away, laughing.

It's done! My parents know about you, and of course they say we're too young. My mother (my father just sits there looking stunned and sad) thinks i should have you adopted.

i will never let you go.

7

One day Emily stood in the doorway to the kitchen while Charlotte brewed up rosehip tea.

'I'm adopted, aren't I?' she said accusingly.

The lid of the small china teapot made a chinking sound.

'Emily! Whatever makes you say that?'

'I am, aren't I?'

Charlotte came over to her. She put both arms round Emily.

'No. No you're not. You're definitely not adopted. I should know – I saw your mother when she was pregnant, and I was there just after you were born. Why on earth do you think that?'

'Oh. Just because. Because she was so old when she had me. And because she didn't have any other children.'

Emily's mother was years older than the other mothers of people her age. Sometimes she was mistaken for Emily's grandmother. She and Charlotte had been at school together, but Charlotte's children were all in their thirties, all with husbands or wives and good jobs, having countless children between them.

'She wanted a child for years. And when you came along at last when she was well past forty, it seemed like a miracle. You've no idea how much you were wanted, Emily.'

'So why didn't she want *my* baby?' said Emily bitterly, shaking

Charlotte away and going to the window where she started fiddling with the coloured glass bottles on the sill. She knocked against a deep blue one; it fell onto the floor and shattered.

Emily walked immediately out of the house.

She walked, unseeing, through the streets until she came to the edge of the town. It perched above a tossing sea of trees. Out there, the birds were held aloft at eye-level in the wind.

She walked away from the lookout, her head down. But even in her anger and misery she noticed the yellow flowers. There was a scattering of them in the rocky patches near the cliffs, and in the back streets. They flourished in all the unpromising dry places where flowers oughtn't to be. Emily bent to pick one, and then another. Some had yellow petals and maroon centres; she didn't know what they were called. Others – also yellow, she recognised them as dandelions – were weeds. All the flowers she was picking were just weeds. In a damper patch she discovered a clump of buttercups.

Soon her hands were full of bright yellow flowers, and Emily stood, uncertain of what to do with them. She kept walking and came to Martin's house, where the front door stood ever open.

She went up the front steps and left the bunch of flowers on the front doormat.

So here we are among clouds. We live close to the sky, on a high hill. You won't remember that some of the first months of your life (because

*even though you're not yet born, i can feel you kicking) were spent in
a small caravan close to the clouds and the stars. We are close to the
weather here. We are the first to feel drops of rain. The moon lights up
our bed at night. In the mornings the new sun slants through the open
doorway, and the light is pink and gold.*

'Someone left me flowers!' said Martin.

'They're just weeds,' said Emily, quietly.

'But pretty ones. Calliopsis, and dandelions.'

She'd trailed after him into the kitchen where the flowers
stood on the kitchen table in a sky-blue vase.

Martin never expressed surprise when Emily turned up.
And he always smiled, as though pleased to see her.

He was just kind, that was why. Emily couldn't imagine
that anyone would be happy to see her, but she was grateful
for his kindness.

'I'm having a party in a couple of weeks,' he told her. 'On
Saturday. It's my birthday and I'd love you to come. It'll just
be a few friends and their kids – nothing big.'

He handed her a hand-made invitation. She looked at it,
then folded it and put it into the pocket of her shirt.

Some days, for Emily, were worse than others. Today she
felt that she was wading through a river filled with silt.

Martin made tea. Sometimes he made hot chocolate, but

he preferred tea. It made him seem old to her, this passion for cups of tea. They took it into the back yard.

The sky was filled with high cloud. Their tea steamed beside them on the path.

'Who is here with us,' said Martin, taking up his notebook and scribbling in it. *A girl, rather sadder than usual today, with brown eyes and an upturned nose and a sprinkling of freckles across her face.*

He stopped, and looked around for more inspiration.

'Two sun skinks,' said Emily in a soft, low voice, astonished at how the words had come so suddenly into her mouth. 'Chasing each other up a wall.'

'One with the end of its tail missing,' added Martin, writing it down.

Emily looked searchingly at him. She wanted to ask him if he'd ever done anything he'd really regretted. But she couldn't say the words out loud, and the moment passed.

While Martin put on a stew to cook in the kitchen, she drifted to Pete's room and lay down on his bed. She was pleased that Pete was at pre-school; she couldn't have borne his scrutiny today. She closed her eyes and fell asleep.

When she woke, Pete was crouched above her, staring intently into her face without blinking.

'Quit it!' she said, pushing him away.

'We've got toast and strawberry jam!' he said.

'I'm not hungry.'

He ran out of the room.

She hauled herself into a sitting position. While she was

still sitting there, Pete ran back into the room with a towel wrapped round his shoulders. 'Do you want to watch me in the bath, Emily?'

'Not really.'

'But I'm not allowed in the bath by myself and Dad's busy!'

When she didn't reply, he coaxed, 'I could sing to you, and you could sit and think. You like sitting and doing nothing.'

She helped Pete undo the buttons of his shirt, and climb out of his trousers. In the bath he whooshed up and down, pretending that he was a whale. Water sloshed all over the floor. Emily sat on the worn lino with her back against the edge of the doorway. The bathroom had two doors – one into the house, and one that led onto the verandah – so there was a leafy view.

When Pete had had enough of being a whale, he sat and sucked on the facewasher. 'You shouldn't drink bathwater,' Emily told him.

'But I like it.' His penis floated in the water like seaweed. He flipped at it, and laughed when it bounced around and bobbed back up to the surface of the water.

'I thought you were going to sing to me.'

'I was, but I forgot the words.'

When Martin called down the hallway that it was time to get out, Pete ignored him.

Emily picked up the towel. 'Come on, Pete.'

'Just a bit longer . . . Emmy – where was I before I was born?'

Emily frowned. 'You should ask Martin that.'

She stood with the towel to lift him from the tub, and wrapped it round his warm, wet body. He put his arms round her neck, and she hauled him out. She closed her eyes for a moment and breathed in the scent of him, then put him down on the ground. But he wouldn't let go.

'You're strangling me,' she said. 'Just stop it, okay?'

Things i love about Matt:

The way he smiles even in his sleep

He is optimistic – always thinks things will turn out for the best

He can cook! Damper in the ashes and pumpkin soup and egg jaffles are his best things

The way he plays his guitar with a little thump a thumpa thump, just like a heartbeat

He puts his hands on my belly when you kick, and the look on his face . . .

When he soaps my back in the shower he always finishes by kissing this little mole on my shoulder

He brings me tea in bed

He's part of you

And too many other things to list but you will find out for yourself

9

'I wish I could introduce you to someone,' said Charlotte one day. 'Someone your own age.'

Charlotte had introduced Emily to several people, but they weren't the sort of people she meant. They were friends of Charlotte's, women of her age, with an interest in books or art or gardening. They came to the house sometimes, where they made room on the table in her tiny kitchen for the endless pots of tea they brewed and the cakes they brought with them. They were noisy, cake-eating women, who laughed a lot and showed too much interest in Emily for her liking. After greeting them, Emily always crept out of the house and stayed away for the rest of the afternoon.

'You need to see people,' said Charlotte, worrying away at Emily's lack of a social life.

'I see people,' said Emily defensively, immediately wishing she hadn't spoken. She didn't want to have to explain to Charlotte about Martin and Pete. Because what sort of friends were they? Martin wasn't the friend *of her own age* that Charlotte envisaged for Emily. He was ten years older than she was. And what did she do at their place? Just sit about in the back yard, or sleep a lot, in Pete's bed.

But to stop Charlotte worrying so much she did tell her about them.

She said that she'd met Martin and Pete one day in the park; it was only a small white lie. She explained that Cat was a nurse and Martin stayed at home to look after Pete. She didn't say that she'd not met Cat yet, because despite Martin asking her to come over on the weekends when Cat was at home, she hadn't wanted to go.

She didn't tell Charlotte about Martin's birthday party, because she didn't know whether she would go yet. Martin had said that it would be very casual, just a few friends with their children, but that seemed to Emily to be far too many people.

She looked for a present for Martin anyway. What she found was a new notebook for him to write down all the creatures he shared the world with: he'd almost filled his current one. Emily covered the notebook with a scrap of golden silk from Thailand, which she'd found as a remnant in a fabric shop. She wrote on the first page, in large curly writing with a gold calligraphy pen she'd found in Charlotte's shed:

A NOTEBOOK TO HANG OUT IN
To Martin, on his birthday,
Luv, Emily

She went to a shop that made chocolates. Emily had seen them in the window, but had never before gone inside. It was an old café, furnished with dark-stained timber counters and tables and chairs similarly sombre. Lamps with old shades threw pools of light upon the tables. The shop reminded her of a church: somewhere dim and holy and hushed.

Emily approached the counter cautiously; apart from buying the silk, it was a long time since she'd been in a shop that wasn't a chain store, where you had to ask for what you wanted. But it gave her a kind of pleasure to select, one at a time, enough chocolates to fill a small box.

'Is it a gift?' asked the assistant, and Emily looked up at her, startled.

'I mean, do you want it gift-wrapped?'

'Oh. Yes, please.'

On the day of the party she was still undecided about whether she would go, but at the last moment she had a quick shower and put on a clean tracksuit. She had thought of looking into her suitcase for a dress, but that would have taken the kind of energy she didn't have.

Several cars were parked in the street outside Martin's house, and a cluster of balloons hung from the railing of the verandah. Voices spilled out from the back yard. The front door was open.

Clutching her presents, Emily made her way slowly down the hallway. A young woman with a baby on her hip was fetching a tray of fruit drinks from the kitchen table; she smiled at Emily in a perky, friendly way before going back out to the garden where the party seemed to be taking place.

Emily stood at the back door and chewed her bottom lip. Instead of stepping out of the house to join the party she went into the laundry, through a door at the back of the kitchen. It was a long, low lean-to at the rear of the building, with another door leading into the back yard – a dark, old place, with concrete tubs and spiderwebs in the corners of the room. Emily peered from the dusty window that was smeared with splashes of soap.

Martin knelt on a rug, pulling the wrapping from a present. He pulled out a snow dome; laughing, he shook it, and kissed the person who'd given it to him in a dramatic and exaggerated way. He had a pair of fairy wings pinned to his back, and they made him look absurd, and emphasised his largeness.

A woman Emily recognised from the photographs as Cat was standing with some other people at a trestle table, arranging plates and cutlery in piles. She had a confident, clever face, and dangly earrings. Her hair was pulled tightly away from her face and caught at the back of her head. She had an air of certainty; she sipped wine and joked with her friends like someone who was absolutely sure of her place in the world.

Pete wrestled on the grass with a pile of other children; they tumbled about like a litter of puppies or kittens. Music came from a portable CD player. It was all noise and movement and laughter, but Emily felt remote from it. She looked down at her clothes. She hadn't even bothered to dress up. In her heart, Emily had known all along that she wouldn't go to the party.

She couldn't bring herself to go out and face all those strange people. She couldn't even face Martin and Pete, who weren't *her* Martin, *her* Pete. They had become different people, and belonged to the people they were with, not with Emily. She was the Emily who wept secret tears and slept for hours in Pete's bed. She had no place at a party.

She put the two gifts that she'd brought onto the sill of the laundry window, and crept out of the house.

That night in bed, Emily thought about what had happened. How could she face people ever again? She couldn't do that; she couldn't walk into a crowd of people, with everyone staring at her, and her standing there unable to say anything.

Emily got out of bed and dressed.

The sky was huge, and the world loomed giant and unfriendly. Emily tucked her chin into her chest and began to walk. It was still early – she'd gone to bed soon after nine – and Charlotte, who was still sitting up listening to quiet music, hadn't heard Emily let herself out the back door.

The leaves on the trees shivered in the wind. Someone passed Emily on the path and said 'Good evening', but she didn't look up, just stumbled a bit, and walked on a little faster. She paused at houses where she could see people through the windows. A woman sat alone holding a book, a reading light shining over her shoulder. Someone came in and put a cup down beside her; the woman looked up gratefully. At another house a child's voice called out something unintelligible. A white cat sat at a darkened windowsill.

The lights in Martin's house were on and there was music coming from the front room. As Emily stood in the street watching, she saw Martin walk across in front of the window.

He didn't look out. He didn't see her, standing in the shadows on the other side of the street.

There was someone with him: Cat ('like the animal!'). Emily saw her walk in front of the window – she watched as Cat turned around and said something. Did Emily hear a laugh?

And then they began to dance, their arms around each other, soft and close and slow.

Emily clenched her hands into her pockets and walked quickly away down the street.

Last night we couldn't sleep, it was so hot – we moved the mattress out onto the grass. The sky was clear and there were lots of stars. Then a breeze came up, and we danced naked in the moonlight, close together, but my belly is so big now that it was kind of awkward. But the dancing was just the best thing.

10

Emily had known that Martin was married, and that he had friends, but that part of his life never seemed real to her. She had only ever seen him in relation to herself and Pete, offering cups of tea, playing with Pete in the park, not minding when she fell asleep at his house in the afternoons, smiling, writing in his notebook while she watched. But he had a whole other life. Why should he bother with someone like her?

Two days after the party, even though his front door was shut when she went past, she knocked. No one answered, but when she pushed at the door it opened, and that seemed like an invitation to go in. Martin never minded: he was the type who always said 'Make yourself at home'. And Emily did, because she felt as much at home at his place as she did at Charlotte's, or anywhere.

She stepped into the house and made her way down the hallway, calling out shyly as she went, but without hope, for the house was obviously deserted. In the kitchen a wooden pepper-grinder stood in the middle of the table. The remains of the birthday cake (chocolate, with the letters *rtin* sitting on the top in thick white piping) sat under a plastic dome-shaped cover. A sharp knife was next to it.

Emily took an upturned glass from the edge of the sink and drew some water from the tap. She heard herself swallow, and the clink of the glass as she returned it to the bench.

I exist, she told herself. *This is me. I am here.*

A bread knife stood upright, poking out of the utensil drainer. She shoved it into a kitchen drawer, along with the knife beside the cake.

After the drawer had slid shut, the silence in the house seemed even more pronounced. She pressed herself against the kitchen sink and looked out the window without seeing. She wished that Martin and Pete had been home. She wished someone other than herself would make a noise. She wished that her own footsteps didn't sound so hollow as she walked back slowly through the house.

Pete's bed was unmade, and a scatter of Lego bricks was spilt across his floor.

She'd never been in Martin's bedroom. Martin and Cat's. The bed had a printed Indian cover with blue and red elephants on it. Emily stood on the striped rug next to it and wondered which side was Martin's.

There was a small chest of drawers on either side of the bed. On top of one was a bottle of massage oil, a copy of *Bridget Jones's Diary*, a pen, and the small covered notebook that Emily had left wrapped up in the laundry on the day of the party. The other table carried a hairbrush, nail scissors, and a bowl with several pairs of earrings in it.

Emily sat down on the side of the bed that had her notebook next to it. She touched its golden silk cover with one finger. It existed, all right. She didn't open it to see if anything had been written in it.

And because it was her habit to sleep in this house, and

because she was suddenly so tired, she lay back against the pillow (did it smell of Martin?) and closed her eyes.

She woke when someone entered the room. It was Cat. She looked exactly as she had at the party – very confident and smooth, and glowing with a kind of inner certainty. She stood just inside the doorway with a look of amazement on her face. Then Pete ran in. 'Emmy! Here you are . . . you didn't come to the party and I waited for you all day!'

'I'm sorry,' Emily whispered, unable to take her eyes from Cat (Cat like the animal; Cat who didn't look too pleased to find a strange girl in her bed).

'I'm sorry,' she said again. She was on her feet. She fled down the hallway and out the front door.

11

Emily felt she would never be able to go to Martin's house again. She could see how peculiar it was, walking into someone's house, falling asleep on their bed. She knew that she didn't behave the way you were meant to. But she knew of no other way to be. This was what she was like now. Better to stay away from other people.

She slept her mornings away. She walked to the lookout and back, the way she had in her pre-Martin and Pete days. She found herself crying for no reason. And then she'd wipe away her tears and get on with doing whatever it was she did next.

A few days later she sat in the park where once she and Martin and Pete had eaten the iceblocks. There was a pigeon huddled on the ground under a tree. Emily sat for a long time and watched it. Another pigeon, probably its mate, stood nearby. The huddled pigeon shifted about from time to time, but its eyes were hooded and sick-looking. When someone walked past, the pigeon that was waiting fluttered into the air.

At some time in the afternoon Emily became aware that the huddled pigeon was no longer alive. Life had leaked slowly from it while she'd been sitting there. She got up and went to kneel beside it. When she lifted it up, its head flopped to one side. The bird was just a loose collection of bones and flesh inside a mass of ruffled feathers.

'Emily.'

She looked up, the lifeless bird cradled in her hands.

'It's dead,' she said.

Martin knelt down beside her. 'Where have you been? I haven't seen you for ages.'

She didn't say anything for a long time, and then – 'I'm sorry I upset Cat,' she said.

'It's okay.'

After a while he added, 'What are you going to do with the bird? Do you want to bury it?'

Emily stared in front of her. Life seemed too sad and futile for her to deal with. 'I've nothing to dig with,' she said. 'Anyway, it's just a bird.'

'Let's put it under these dead leaves over here. Under the bush, where no one walks.'

After they'd concealed the bird, Emily stood with her hands hanging at her sides. Without the small bundle to hold, she had no idea what to do with them. They didn't even feel like her hands.

Martin took her by the shoulders, gently, the way he held Pete sometimes when he was getting too speedy for his own good, and led her over to the path.

They passed a young man. Emily had often seen him walking the streets. His hair was matted and long, and his feet were bare. His skin had a raw, weathered look to it. He never smiled.

When they were well past him, Martin said, 'His eyes are so blue.'

He found them a seat. 'Sit down here and watch people with me. It's always surprising what you see.'

In ten minutes they saw a child with a dummy stuck in its mouth being wheeled in a pram by an old woman in slippers, a black dog with short legs going for a walk on its own ('A very busy dog,' said Martin, 'probably late for an appointment'), and a man Emily recognised as the shark man (though she didn't tell Martin this). He wasn't muttering anything that day, but he gave them a swift, angry glance as he went past.

Martin said, 'What is it, Emily? Why are you always so sad?'

She said, 'I did something . . .'

He was looking at her.

'Something terrible.'

'You can tell me,' he said. 'Nothing shocks me.'

She said, looking at the ground, 'I had a baby. A baby girl.' She looked up at him to see his reaction.

Martin was looking at her with a face full of tenderness and dismay. And he didn't rearrange his expression to one that he felt suitable for the occasion. 'A baby,' he said softly.

'I couldn't look after her properly,' said Emily, surprised at how easily she could tell him this, something she had never said to anyone. 'And I was so scared I'd do something dreadful to her that I had to leave her.

'What kind of mother does that?' she asked him.

12

Emily took Martin back and introduced him to Charlotte; she saw how Charlotte, while reaching out to shake his hand with a smile, sized him up behind her cool, vague exterior. In the kitchen, Emily poured glasses of cranberry juice. Martin drank slowly, gazing at the coloured glass bottles on the windowsill. They sat for a while in the cluttered living room, and he looked at the picture of the angel in the green dress, and smiled. 'Chagall,' he said affectionately, as if he'd just met an old friend. 'The man who painted that picture,' he added, when he saw Emily's puzzled expression. He nodded at another print, of a man and a woman floating in an embrace above the ordinary domesticity of their living room, the woman with a bunch of flowers in her hand. 'Love can be like that.'

Emily looked again at the picture. The woman had a most tender and expectant expression as she raised her face to be kissed; both she and her lover hovered gracefully, gravity pulling at their feet, their bodies fluid like lengths of ribbon falling to the ground.

'How do you learn to do that?' she said. 'Float above everything so effortlessly?'

'In a radiant and ecstatic way? If I ever get hold of the instructions I'll give them to you.'

As he left he said, at the gate, 'I do think Charlotte's house needs more in it, don't you? It's a bit bare as it is. Just a bit more furniture, a few more books and pictures, a couple of ornaments here and there, might make it look more lived-in, don't you think?'

Emily giggled, and Martin kissed her on the cheek and departed. He turned to say, 'Come round to see us!' and she watched him walk all the way up the street.

'Isn't he a bit old for you?' said Charlotte later.

'No,' said Emily, with a rising inflection. 'He's just turned twenty-seven.

'And he's *married*, with a five-year-old child.

'And we're *just friends*. It's okay to have a guy for a friend, isn't it?'

That night, they ate dinner off their laps watching television; macaroni cheese, in hand-made blue bowls made by one of Charlotte's friends. While they ate they watched *The Simpsons*, which Charlotte said she didn't really *get*. It didn't matter to Emily what show was on, she watched all television these days without seeing or hearing it properly. She kept her eyes fixed on the screen and forked macaroni into her mouth without tasting it; it was soft and mushy and comforting. And all the time, on the walls above them, the lovers levitated and the angel in the green dress flew with her posy of flowers.

Afterwards, Charlotte switched off the television and picked up Emily's empty bowl. Emily sat on a cushion on the floor, leaning back against the sofa, staring at the pictures on the wall. 'Chagall,' she said slowly. 'I didn't know that painter was called Chagall.'

Charlotte paused at the door to the kitchen with her hands full of crockery. 'When I was your age, one of the nuns at school, Sister Charles, introduced me to him. That was pretty amazing for a nun in those days – he isn't what you'd call a traditional religious painter. But he *is* religious, in his own wonderful way.'

Charlotte clattered about in the kitchen. When she returned she plopped down on the sofa behind Emily and lifted Emily's hair into her hands. 'This needs cutting,' she said. 'How long since you've been to the hairdresser?'

Emily shrugged, and Charlotte picked up a brush from the side table. 'And so tangled!' she said, as she began to brush it. When she'd finished she leaned forward and kissed Emily lightly on the cheek. 'I can take you for a trim this week, if you'd like.'

When Emily didn't reply, Charlotte peered at her face and said, 'Yes?'

'I don't like hairdressers,' said Emily. 'Any more.'

'Oh. Okay. How about I cut it for you? I have some hair scissors. Would you mind me doing it?'

'No,' said Emily, in a low voice. 'I mean, I wouldn't mind if you did it.'

Next day, Charlotte sat Emily on a chair in the yard with a towel round her neck, and started to clip.

'When your mum and I were at boarding school together the girls were forbidden to touch each other. No hugs and kisses or hanging off each other the way girls do these days. I think the nuns were afraid we'd get unnaturally interested in each other or something.' She laughed.

'But, away from our families, we craved to be touched. The only thing that was considered to be all right was brushing each other's hair. A lot of hair-brushing went on, I can tell you.

'There were so many hang-ups. You were either a good girl or a bad girl.

'We were good girls. The bad girls sneaked out to meet boys – boys from the nearby boys' school, or boys they'd met in town. They used to talk about how far they'd gone with them – quite far, in many cases. There's nothing quite like being educated by nuns to make girls keen on sex. They make it seem so special and holy and forbidden – too much of a temptation altogether, I can tell you. I think I was good because I was too afraid of the consequences.

49

'I secretly admired the bad girls.

'The most daring thing your mother and I did was the day we took off our clothes and swam in the creek while we were on a cross-country race. No one saw us – we found a hidden part of the creek just a little way from the track. It was all shaded and secluded, all soft silt on the bottom, and overhung by huge old trees. And we floated there for ages with our boobs bobbing on top of the water like balloons, while dozens of girls thundered past. It felt wonderful. Do you know it was the first time I'd seen another girl naked – we always undressed with our backs to everyone.

'We were the last to get back that day – and our hair was all damp and stringy, and Sister Cyril looked at us suspiciously, but we didn't get found out.'

Charlotte brushed Emily's newly trimmed hair free of loose ends.

'She never told me that story.'

'Well, she wouldn't, would she? She always was a bit stuffy. Took me a lot of persuading to get her to take off her clothes.'

Emily hadn't bothered to have her hair cut for a long time. Nor had she trimmed her fingernails; she bit them down if they annoyed her. When her toenails got too long she snipped them off with paper scissors.

Emily, who had once loved her body, never thought about it now. She no longer looked at herself in the mirror (and it had once pleased her to see herself reflected back). She often

50

didn't bother to clean her teeth. She dressed in anything that came to hand – usually an old tracksuit.

That night, in the dark, she ran her hands over her body. Once, she'd often touched herself with delight. Now, she felt detached, and it gave her no pleasure. She could feel that she was thinner now than she'd ever been. The bones of her hips stuck out, and her belly dipped, concave like a hammock, surprisingly still firm after being stretched by pregnancy.

Every one of her ribs stood out. Her breasts were small.

You might never have known that she'd had a baby.

Emily took one of her nipples between her fingers and squeezed. Eventually, a very small bead of milk came to the surface. She licked it from her finger. It tasted sweet, and thin, and warm.

When i look at my baby i feel nothing, and i'm scared.

Two

1

When Martin left Emily at her front gate, he strode away with his arms swinging freely, his chest open and expansive. He felt the air passing in and out of his lungs, easy and slow. He was pleased that he'd found her again.

When he got to his place the front door was shut, and he took a key from his pocket and unlocked it. Cat kept the front door closed, but Martin always left it open, and the back door, too, in all but the worst weather, or at night. It wasn't so much the flow of air that he wanted, but the sense that the house was open to the world, and that everything could flow through it. He hated houses to be isolated, self-contained boxes. He wanted to feel that anyone in the world might come to his door. He remembered the day that Emily had first stood there, looking ready to flee. If the door had been closed, she might never have knocked.

As he made his way down the hallway, Cat called from the

bedroom, and he went in. She was sitting at the dressing table, doing things to her face. He dropped down onto the bed and lay with his hands behind his head. 'You going out?' he asked. It was obvious from the care she was taking with her appearance that she was, though he often wondered why she bothered. To him, she looked nicer in plain old everyday clothes – jeans and a sweater and brightly coloured sneakers.

'Don't you remember? We're meant to be going to Michelle and Damien's for dinner.'

'That's cool. I'm ready when you are.'

Cat kept looking at herself in the mirror. 'Pete's had a bath but he's probably dirty again by now. Where were you all afternoon?'

Martin sat up and leaned on one elbow. 'I met Emily.' He stopped. Then he said, 'I found her, Cat. She was sitting in the park . . . Cat, she told me that she's had a baby, but that she left it – I haven't asked all the details yet, but imagine how she's feeling . . .'

Cat turned to look at him. He saw that she was annoyed with him, but all she said was, 'She's a very strange girl.' She said it cautiously, as though she was keeping another comment in check. 'When I found her sleeping on our bed that after-noon . . .' She frowned. 'It's all a bit much, really.'

When he didn't reply, Cat said, 'Why do you encourage her? I mean, she's such a kid. A troubled one, by the sound of it.'

Martin thought for a moment. 'She needs people to talk to,' he said. 'Some place to go. And Pete likes her. Most of the time.'

'I like her,' he added decisively.

What he didn't tell Cat was that, despite the difference in their ages, he felt a kind of affinity with Emily that couldn't be explained by a similarity of interests or anything rational at all. It was simply that deep down he felt they were made of the same stuff. He felt at ease with her, despite her silences and moodiness.

'Besides,' he said with mock sorrow, 'Pete and I have trouble getting play dates. She's someone for us to be with. We're almost outcasts, otherwise.'

'Trouble getting play dates!' said Cat, plonking herself down on top of him and wrestling his arms above his head.

'It's true! I'm just not one of the girls. I've tried, God knows. But they're in a sort of club, with their tidy cargo pants and . . . and their girl talk. And they talk about their kids in a different way than I do.'

'They came to your party!' said Cat, releasing him.

'Yes, but that was because it was a party. And because you were there.'

'Anyway, what about that hippy woman who used to come over – what was her name? Amber?' Cat fished some shoes out of the wardrobe.

Martin groaned. 'Amber! Don't you remember? She didn't believe in saying "no" at all. And little Magenta was a biter. Pete hated her. He prefers Emily, he really does.'

'And despite her also being a girl, she's okay to be with?' said Cat, looping the shoe straps over her heels.

'Yes,' said Martin softly. He went to get a fresh shirt. They were arrayed in neat piles in the cupboard. It was Cat who kept their cupboards tidy. She was so *organised*. It was one of the things that had attracted him to her – her capability and certainty. They'd met when he'd seen a car pulled up beside the road with the bonnet up. He'd been passing on his motorbike and stopped to give a hand. And there was Cat, dressed in old jeans, triumphant at having successfully wrangled with a dirty sparkplug. Her hands had been covered in grease; she hadn't needed his help at all. He often thought of what she'd be like at work; in the operating theatre she'd assist without flinching, peering into the bloodied interior of the patient on the table as if it was an interesting problem that needed solving.

'Anyway,' he said, pausing at the doorway to watch her check her face in the mirror again, 'I don't see why we should always have to like the same people.

'Come on, Pete!' he called, going out into the hall. 'We've got to be somewhere soon!' He found Pete in the sandpit in the dusky garden, and took him through to the bathroom to wash his hands.

'Come on, let's get you into your pyjamas. You'll probably want to go to sleep before we get home.'

'I hate going to sleep at other people's places,' said Pete.

Martin went to Pete's room and threw some toys into a bag, then almost collided with Cat in the hallway, as she came out carrying a bottle of wine she'd just grabbed from the fridge. Without speaking, they crammed themselves into the car and drove off.

They arrived home several hours later with Pete asleep in the back seat. Martin carried him, warm and floppy, into the house, and tucked him into bed. Martin thought that after Pete had grown up and left home, he would remember times like this as some of the happiest of his life.

But later, when Cat had fallen asleep and he stood at their bedroom window staring out at the dark, it wasn't his family he was thinking of, it was Emily. In the park that afternoon she'd asked him, 'What sort of mother does that?' He hadn't been able to give her an answer – but then, it had been one of those questions, full of despair and self-hatred, that didn't require an answer.

2

She arrived two mornings later while he was in the middle of doing the washing. Standing in the damp laundry with piles of clothes all over the floor, he heard a sound at the front of the house through the grinding noise of the machine. He went out into the hall and she was standing at the open front door the way she had that first time, looking uncertain and ready to run away again.

'Hey!' he said. 'Emily! Come in . . .'

'You don't mind?'

'No. It's good to see you.' He had to go down the length of the hall and meet her where she stood on the threshold before she would step inside. But she wouldn't look at him, and he took her through to the laundry where he pulled a load of clothes from the machine. Without speaking, she helped him peg the washing onto the line, and then they sat in the thin sunlight on the back step. Emily stared broodingly at the path.

Martin got up. 'Do you know what?' he said. 'Pete's at pre-school and now I've done the washing I'm through with my chores for the day. I feel like taking a holiday – d'you want to do something?'

'Yeah,' she said, and her smile was as strained as the sun attempting to shine through the clouds. So he packed a small backpack with water bottles and fruit and as they went down the hall he handed her the rainbow hat from the peg. She crammed it onto her head as though she didn't care how it looked, and he had to stop himself straightening it and turning up the brim for her. He wanted to give her a hug and somehow make it all better, the way he did with Pete some-times, but he couldn't take that liberty. She was too old for that, and she was a girl, and she wasn't his child.

So what he did was walk with her. He took her to the far side of town and down a bush track into the valley, climbing down steps cut into the rocky cliff face. As they descended, the forest became damper and darker. The air was clean and cool. At the bottom of the valley he came to a causeway where the path crossed a small creek. From here on, it was his secret place, off the track. He took her up beside the creek, where water trickled over rocks and moss silenced their footsteps.

He brought her to a pool with a small waterfall at the top

of it. They sat on adjoining stones and sipped water from the bottles that Martin took from his pack. He handed her an apple, and she bit into it.

Martin removed his shoes and went to sit at the side of the pool with his feet in the water. 'Try it,' he said, 'it's not as cold as you might think.'

When she didn't respond, Martin went over and started to unlace her shoes, as if she was a child. Removing them from her feet gently, he tucked the socks inside and placed them neatly on a rock. Then he took her hand and led her to the pool, and they sat on the edge together

She said, 'My mother rang up this morning. I couldn't talk to her. I never can.' She looked at him. 'I have nothing to say to her.'

Martin made no comment. Then he said, 'Can you tell me about your baby? What's her name – and who's looking after her now?'

Emily thought for a moment. She said tenderly, 'Her name's Mahalia. Her father's looking after her. His name's Matt.'

She looked away and examined a leaf that she picked up from the ground.

'And this Matt – he's all right doing this? He can look after her okay?'

Emily nodded. 'Better than I could,' she said.

There followed one of those silences where Martin couldn't think what else to say – he didn't want to seem to be prying and Emily didn't volunteer anything else. 'How agile are you?' he said eventually.

Emily looked up at him with such a look of surprised anticipation that he got up and led her over the rocks that straddled the creek. She turned out to be very light on her feet, and followed him readily as he leapt from boulder to boulder. They came to a twisted fig tree on a rocky outcrop, and as they clambered past it, Martin took hold of her hand. He felt how soft it was, the bones in it.

'Look,' he said. 'The tree's hollow.'

She stood on tiptoe and looked into it and smiled. He told her that it was a good nest for a possum; it was scattered with leaves and twigs and bark. After peering down into the tree they both looked up at the sky where it showed through the canopy. The rapid change in perspective gave him a feeling of vertigo; he closed his eyes and when he looked at her she was standing there patiently waiting for him.

They moved on, and came to a part of the creek where the rushing water made many layers of sound, with high splashing notes underlaid occasionally with deep gurgles, as the water ran on a hidden, complicated path under the stones. He sat her down on a rock as though he was conducting her to a seat in a concert hall, then went away and left her alone with the music of the water. He went back to the first rockpool where the water also rushed, though in a much more roaring and straightforward way. He waited for her there, and his head was full of the sound of the water, and it was that sound that was important, rather than the look of the water, or the trees, or the sky, or anything.

After a while he saw her picking her way down the creek.

When she got within a metre of him she lay down on the ground and closed her eyes. She said in a slow, even voice, 'I have this grey sludgy feeling that is there most of the time. And it makes me strange, and say strange things, and not know how to behave with people. It's because the world I'm living in isn't the same as the world they're in. It makes it hard to connect.

'You're okay because I know you, and you make allowances for me. You know to just keep talking anyway, and sometimes when I'm with you and Pete there's this thin, silvery-blue opening where I can see the place where everyone else is. And sometimes I think that if I'm patient then one day the crack will get wider and wider, until the blue is the whole world. And I'll be me again.'

There was nothing but the sound of the rushing water, and after a while she stretched and got to her feet. Martin stood up too, and without speaking they made their way back up into the world.

Afterwards, he remembered the look of her as she lay there on the ground.

She'd had her hair cut since the last time he'd seen her. It was shorter and blunter, and she held it away from her forehead with a broad stretchy hairband. He saw how unhealthy and pallid the skin on her face was – almost grey. Her forehead was dotted with tiny pimples. She looked pathetically young to have had a baby.

She wore the same old trackpants and fleecy top she always wore. The pants had slipped down over her hips and the top rode up as she lay with her arms above her head, leaving her middle exposed. He thought how transparent her skin, how mottled with cold, and threaded with fine blue veins. He saw the slenderness of her waist, and the steady rhythm of her breathing.

3

Martin didn't tell Cat that he'd spent the day with Emily in the forest. He wasn't sure why he kept it from her. Nothing had *happened* between them. But if nothing had happened, why did he have such a feeling of expectancy each day? He always half expected to find Emily standing at the open door. But she didn't come.

In the meantime there was his ordinary, everyday life: pegging the washing out to dry, enjoying the smell of fresh sheets; seeing Pete hurtling into the child-care centre in the mornings and hurtling out just as fast when he was picked up in the afternoons; making a snack with him when they got home; eating it together in the back yard. There was curling up behind Cat in the early morning, every morning, a special, blessed part of each day; reaching over to take her hand while she slept.

The air was balmy, and it made even more sense to keep

all the doors and windows open. But a bird got caught in the house; a little brown honeyeater that couldn't find the way out. He finally released it by throwing a teatowel over it and cupping its small beating body inside his hands. Then there was the mouse that had crept into the kitchen and lived there somewhere, which he fed by putting a few crumbs on a saucer in the corner. But when he found it running around on the bench one day, about to get into the bread (it slunk away, low and lean, its belly flat to the ground), he caught it in a tunnel trap and released it into the forest. There was the spider that lived above the laundry tubs and stood guard over an egg sac. There was the yellow robin in the lemon tree, looking just like a lemon; it looked at him with its bright eye and flew away. He recorded all of this in the silk-covered book that Emily had given him.

And then one day she was there. It was an ordinary morning, a non-pre-school day. He and Pete were making a chocolate cake. Pete had licked out the bowl, and had some-how got chocolate mixture all over his fringe ('I wanted to see what it would be like to actually lick it out, Dad, and not use the spoon'), and the cake was in the oven. And there was Emily at the front door, then in the kitchen, staring almost without comprehension at a wooden spoon full of raw cake-mix that Pete had thrust into her hands, and fending off Pete's ques-tions as to where she'd been. 'Nowhere, Pete,' she said. 'I never go anywhere. I've just been . . . *about.*'

She seemed very cool and calm, and almost happy. They went out into the back yard, and Martin got his guitar, a steel-stringed acoustic that he seldom played any more; it felt as if he hadn't played it for years. And he sat on the grass and played her a tune he hadn't thought of in a long time, a tune he associated with the time years ago when he played in the band. Emily listened with a smiling, wistful, distracted expression on her face, and Martin said when he'd finished, 'It's a pretty little tune, isn't it?'

She said, 'Matt plays the guitar. Matt . . . Mahalia's father? But he plays bass.'

That was all she said. They sat there in the sun with Pete buzzing round them while Martin played another tune.

After that, Emily came round almost every day. She took to coming into the house again without knocking, and he could gauge how she was by the manner of her arrival. If she was having a good day she pinged the bell on the bicycle in the hallway to warn him she was on her way; on bad days she slunk into the kitchen without speaking and seemed crushed, scarcely able to move.

On a good day she might take Pete for a walk to the corner shop and come back with packets of mixed lollies; she ate lunch with fastidious pleasure, picking up her food in her fingers and afterwards licking them ostentatiously. Other times she would weep at apparently nothing, walk into a branch of the lemon tree and scratch her face, or accidentally drop a plate on the floor, leave the house, and not come back for days.

She could sit for ages not saying anything, staring straight ahead, and there was something fierce and desperate in her expression. She was like someone in a silent, continuous battle with herself.

They sometimes sat in the garden and talked about nothing in particular. Afterwards, he couldn't even remember what they'd said. A tree in the garden dropped pink blossoms over the path. Sometimes one tumbled while he watched, and it was like the soft, sad sound of her occasional laughter.

4

He accepted three days' casual teaching with a Year Three class. He liked to do things with his temporary classes that were easy and fun, so that day they looked for frogs in the drain behind the school (and found none), and then he gave them a photocopied diagram of a frog, and got them to label all the parts of a frog's anatomy from a similar picture he drew on the board. He got them to colour in the frog, and they got so keen on art that he found a whole lot of stuff in the store-room and they made collages of the animals they'd like to be. He'd brought in his acoustic guitar and they sang songs. He read them a story called *Amos and Boris* about a whale and a mouse who were great friends, and they discussed the importance of loyalty and friendship and how you didn't need to be exactly like someone to have a great affinity with them. He got the children to lie down on mats on the floor and taught them how to close their eyes and relax. He watched how some settled down immediately and even fell asleep, and some wriggled and squirmed and opened one eye and giggled, or scratched their noses.

He loved all of them – the ones who came up to him in the playground and put their hands in his, tangling their hot, sweaty little fingers with his own, and those who came up to him earnestly to tell him something, their breath smelling of bananas and peanut butter, and the ones who concentrated so intently on what they were doing that they appeared lost to the rest of the world.

Martin preferred the classroom to the staffroom, where most of the teachers seemed jaded and weary with life. He found few kindred spirits in school staffrooms, though there was often at least one teacher (usually a woman) who chatted to him in a friendly way, or gave him a conspiratorial glance.

It was at the end of one day while the children were lying on the floor relaxing that Martin found the time to think about Emily. The other day, she'd said that even though her parents wanted her to give the baby away, she and Matt had always planned to keep it. 'We thought that if we just loved her enough, everything would be all right. How dumb was that?

'I hated myself. Because I was weak when she needed me to be strong.'

He remembered when Pete was born, the first time he'd

held him. He wanted nothing bad to ever happen to him, he wanted to look after him forever. He remembered cupping that tiny head in his hands, where it fitted perfectly. But you couldn't protect your children from everything. Or perhaps from anything much at all.

That afternoon, after collecting Pete from pre-school, he arrived home to find Emily sitting on the front steps. Inside the house, she curled up on the chair in the living room, and when he brought her in a cup of hot chocolate she'd fallen asleep. He covered her with a blanket, noticing how meekly her feet rested one on top of the other. She had a secret mole at the back of her ankle. She didn't stir even when Pete turned the television on softly for *Play School*, and he and Pete sat there beside her while she slept.

She was still sleeping when Cat arrived home. Martin was in the kitchen preparing the dinner when he heard the front door bang shut. Then Cat was there with her workday eager face. She threw down her bag next to the table and kissed him. 'We've got a visitor?' she said.

'She's not staying . . .'

And then Emily stood at the doorway, drowsy and rumpled. She rubbed her forehead, and then took her hand away and stared at it, as though seeing it for the first time.

'Emily – hey!'

She looked up, as though she hadn't known that anyone

was there. 'Hello? . . . I, um, think I fell asleep.' She gestured towards the living room. 'Better be getting home.'

'Okay,' said Martin. 'I'll see you out. Actually . . . have you met Cat?'

The two of them stood on either side of the kitchen, staring at him. Cat smooth and golden and definite, Emily fuzzy and freckled and astonished-looking.

'Kind of,' said Emily. 'Well, not properly . . . I'd better be getting back. Charlotte . . . my godmother,' she explained to Cat, 'will be wondering where I am.'

Martin went with her to the front door. 'Does she mind?' whispered Emily, as he opened it for her.

'You being here? No – course not.' He reached out and squeezed her arm.

And then she was down the front steps and gone without looking back.

When he got back to the kitchen, Cat said, 'Why don't you invite her to lunch one Saturday?'

'Lunch . . .' said Martin. 'I don't think "lunch" as such, in the way you mean, is the kind of thing she does.'

'What – she doesn't eat?'

'Well, of course she does . . .'

'It's a bit odd, her coming round here all the time when I don't even know her – don't you think it's reasonable that we should at least meet properly?'

'Sure it is.'

But he knew that a formal invitation might throw Emily; simply dropping in when she needed or wanted to was more her style.

'I'll ask her when I see her,' he said.

Later that night, after Pete was in bed, Martin sat in the kitchen playing his guitar while Cat wiped down the kitchen benches. She seemed stern and remote, far too preoccupied with the housework. He strummed softly, one ear on the music, and one on the music of his own heart, which suddenly, more than anything needed to take Cat out to the back yard and dance in the moonlight.

'Dance with me, Cat?'

She didn't reply.

'Out in the garden? There's practically a full moon,' he said.

'Okay,' said Cat lightly. 'Just wait till I finish cleaning the sink.'

'Oh, c'mon,' he said.

'Done.' She threw the sponge down.

Cat wasn't the most romantic girl he'd ever met, but she would dance with him anywhere and any time. She had perfect rhythm, even without music, and she knew how to dance close and slow. That night there was a lot of moonlight to dance in, and a wonderful coldness to the air.

'Do you know what?' he said. 'I've been thinking. I'd like to teach properly. Full-time. It'd be great to get to know a group of kids really well and see them progress.'

'What about Pete?'

'He'll be at school next year. And if you wanted to, you could have another baby and stay home . . . we could swap for a while. How about it?'

Cat didn't say anything, but he could sense her considering it. 'I don't know that I'd want to give up my place at the hospital,' she said after a while, without sounding totally convinced.

There was very little sound to distract them while they danced – a car moving slowly down the street, a dog barking in someone's yard – and Martin felt a great sense of rightness and peace. Everything was cool air and moonlight and the scent and softness of Cat's skin. Then Martin saw a figure standing in the back doorway watching them, a small dark shape against the light from the house.

He broke off. 'Pete,' he said. 'What are you doing up?'

'Getting a drink of water. What are *you* guys doing?'

'Dancing,' replied Cat. 'You know we like dancing.'

She took Pete inside and Martin heard her getting him some water and taking him back to bed. He thought with anxiety about Emily and what it might be like, all of them having lunch together (a weekday lunch with him was always a casual, scrappy affair, and often Emily didn't feel like eating much at all).

When Cat arrived back she took up her place in his arms, but the soundless music they'd been dancing to – the music that had made their movements fluid and effortless – had disappeared somehow. He began by treading on her toe ('Sorry . . .') and then when they tried to start dancing they were hopelessly out of step.

72

Cat stopped. 'Let's start again.'

But the mood was lost. Shrugging, Cat dropped his hand. 'I think I can hear Pete again,' she murmured, and went inside, leaving him alone in the dark garden.

The door was open but Emily knocked, the day she came to lunch. Martin had been listening for her, and walked down the hallway to greet her with a feeling of apprehension. She stood in a short red dress with a mauve cardigan over the top even though the day was warm. Her legs were bare. She carried a huge bunch of roses and ferns which almost obscured her face, so he couldn't read how she was feeling.

'From Charlotte's garden,' she said, thrusting them at him, but he ushered her through to the kitchen so she could give them to Cat herself. Once divested of them she seemed unsure what to do with her hands. He gave her a glass of apple juice, but when he passed it over she didn't grasp it properly and it tipped, sending juice splattering all over the floor.

'Oh . . . I'm sorry. So sorry.'

Cat wiped up the juice. 'It's good to meet you properly at last, Emily . . .' she said, but what she was about to say next was interrupted by Pete. He burst in from where he'd been playing in the backyard, lurched towards Emily and kissed her on her bare knee before catapulting away again, up the hallway to his room. Emily stood helplessly, looking as though she wanted to follow him.

'You can go up to Pete's room if you like,' Martin told her, and she gave him a grateful glance. When he followed a bit later to call them for lunch, she was lying on her back on the floor with her arm shielding her eyes. Pete played with his Lego next to her and talked. He was saying, 'Do you ever think that you might be dreaming or imagining you're alive?' This was Pete's latest thing.

Emily replied slowly, 'All the time, Pete, all the time.'

'Are you two ready for lunch?' said Martin.

Out in the kitchen Martin steered Emily to her seat. She seemed so dreamy that she needed to be guided. Sinking onto the chair, Emily knocked a fork onto the floor; she and Martin both bent to pick it up, and she smiled at him as though he was a stranger, a bright, empty, polite smile.

'So, you're from the north coast, Emily?' said Cat, putting down a basket of garlic bread.

'Yes, I am.' Emily pushed her hair behind her ears and looked at Cat earnestly, like someone having a job interview.

'It's lovely up there,' said Cat. 'Before I met Martin, a girl-friend and I went to Byron Bay on the train, and slept on the beach under the stars.'

Emily smiled politely, tucked her elbows in as though she was remembering her best manners, and dug her fork into the slice of quiche that Martin had put on her plate. 'I did that once,' she said. 'The parents of one of the girls at school had a beach house there. We went to the New Year's Eve parade and got really ripped – almost passed out. Slept the night on the beach instead of going back to the house.' Her voice was soft and dull and matter-of-fact, as though there was no emotion attached to that event. She sipped a glass of juice, and Martin saw that she'd mashed her quiche into crumbs and not eaten a bit. He looked at Cat and she shrugged, and everyone continued to eat in silence. Pete looked at them all and took it all in with big eyes. 'I hate eggs,' he said, pushing away his plate. 'Did you know they come out of chooks' bums?'

Lunch took very little time, and as Martin started to stack plates, Pete tugged Emily to her feet and dragged her away to his room.

'What on earth do you ever find to talk to her about?' said Cat.

'What do you mean?'

'Is she always like that?' said Cat.

'Not quite.'

'Quite?' said Cat. 'You mean, just a little bit?'

'Well, sometimes. She can be funny and charming.'

Cat gave him an *Oh really* look. 'She needs help. Can't you see there's something not quite right with her?'

'I know. She's unhappy. But she's dealing with it in her own way . . .'

'I worry about Pete with her. He told me the other day they walked to the shop and bought lollies. Martin . . . how can you trust her with Pete crossing roads? – she seems so . . . *out* of it!'

Martin found himself bristling, but he bit his tongue. 'I'll go and tell them dessert's almost ready,' he said, as Cat took a chocolate cake from under its cover and reached into the fridge for chocolate and cream.

He saw that Emily was lying on Pete's floor again. 'Do you need a sleep, Emmy, do you?' said Pete, solicitously, putting his face close to hers and staring with unblinking eyes.

'Pete, just leave it,' she said, pushing him away and rolling onto her side.

'Sometimes I hate you,' he said. 'I think you're a pooey bum.' He upended a box full of plastic blocks onto the floor with a crash.

'Chocolate cake!' announced Martin. 'Anyone want any?'

Pete ran out of the room at once, and Martin squatted down beside Emily. 'How're you going?' he said.

'Okay,' she said in a little voice. He smiled, and squeezed her shoulder. She closed her eyes again.

'Come out soon,' he said.

In the kitchen, Cat gave him a bowl of cream to whip and started grating a block of dark chocolate.

'You didn't answer me,' she said. '*Do* you think it's okay for her to take Pete out on the roads?'

Martin paused. Pete had gone to play in the garden and seemed to be out of earshot.

'Someone has to give her a chance sometime,' he said, knowing that it sounded feeble.

'Maybe,' said Cat, sarcastically. 'But with *our* child?'

Martin beat the cream so fiercely it turned as stiff as butter.

'Okay,' he conceded. 'I won't let her take him out to the shops again.'

He thought he heard a sound near the doorway that led into the hall, but he went on. 'Don't you remember being that age?' he said, his face incredulous. 'Because I do. Didn't *you* ever stuff up?'

He slathered cream over the top of the cake.

'Shit!' said Cat.

'What?'

'I've grated my knuckles along with this damn chocolate.'

Martin heard the sound at the doorway again and he turned as if to go out. But he went to Cat and took her hand to see what she'd done.

'I'll be fine,' she said, shaking him away. 'I'm a nurse, remember?'

When Pete ran in clamouring for cake, Martin went to get Emily, but Pete's room was empty. At the front door step he found a scrap of paper with a flower from the garden on top of it.

In crayon was written:

Thanks for inviting me.
It was a lovely lunch.
i have to go.
Emily.

That night, as he found himself thinking about Emily, Cat rolled over to turn off the light and put her arm round him. She said, 'Just remember that *we're* your family, Martin. Us, me and Pete.'

6

She didn't come round again after the day of the lunch.

One day it was so hot that Pete wanted to go to the pool. 'Can we take Emmy?' he asked, pushing his swimming things into a bag. So they went to see if she was home.

It was early afternoon, and Emily, who answered the door, was ruffled and frowsy as though they'd woken her from sleep.

'Emily, hi.' Martin was shy, unsure of what sort of mood she'd be in, or even if he and Pete would be welcome. 'We were on our way to the pool. Would you like to come?'

'I – I don't have any togs,' Emily said.

Charlotte came up behind her. 'I have some bathers that Ruby left here.' She disappeared to the back of the house and came out dangling a red swimming costume by its straps. 'My granddaughter's,' she told Martin. 'She's only twelve, but Emily's so tiny . . .'

Emily took the costume and went to change. She came out looking hot and flustered. If she had the swimming costume on it didn't show, because she was dressed in a tracksuit, top and bottom, far too warm for the hot weather.

At the pool she lay in the shade fully dressed, and it was only when Pete urged her to come into the water that she pulled off the tracksuit quickly, revealing the red costume underneath. She ran to the edge of the pool and dived in.

Afterwards, they all lay like lizards on the warm concrete surrounding the pool, not speaking, basking in the warmth. And then they all went into the water again, staying until Pete started to shiver. His mouth turned blue. So Martin pulled him from the water and wrapped him in a towel, and took him to the kiosk to buy iceblocks. They lay on the hot concrete again, Pete still swathed in the towel like a cocoon.

'Dad?' said Pete. 'Where was I before I was born?'

'I've told you,' said Martin. 'In Cat's tummy.'

'I know that! I mean . . . where was I before that?'

'You've got me there,' said Martin. 'That's a really big question, Pete. I don't know.'

'Because I must have always *been* here, somewhere.'

'Maybe,' said Emily, 'you were in the same place you'll be after you die.'

'Where's that?'

'I don't know,' she said grudgingly, finishing her iceblock and lying back down on her stomach on the concrete. 'It depends on what you believe.'

Pete shucked off his towel and headed back into the water. 'Stay where I can watch you,' Martin called to him.

'Hey,' he said to Emily. 'I'm sorry that lunch the other week wasn't so great for you.'

She shrugged and didn't look at him.

Martin had never before seen Emily with her arms uncovered. Even on the day she'd come to lunch in the red dress, she'd worn a thin knitted cardigan over the top. Now she lay fully stretched out in the sun. The skin of her inner arms was soft and pale like a fish's belly. And it was covered with a network of fine, pale scars.

Martin reached over and ran his finger over them. 'Emily,' he asked softly, 'what are these?'

'Nothing,' she said defensively, twitching away.

'Emily, you can tell me . . .'

'It's none of your business!' she said, reaching for the tracksuit top. She put it on and sat on the concrete with her knees pulled up to her chest and her arms wrapped tight like a straitjacket.

Martin got up and went to call Pete. *If that was the way she wanted it . . .*

'Pete, come on,' he called. 'It's time to go home.'

'Oh, Da – ad!'

'Come on, you've had enough – and I want to get home to do stuff.

'See you, Emily,' he said, but with less warmth than usual. He could feel it in his voice.

'Maybe,' she said.

She half turned as he walked away and gave a sort of gesture of farewell.

The trouble with Emily was . . . (he found himself starting a lot of his thoughts with *The trouble with Emily*) . . . was that he never quite knew when she'd turn up, and when she did, it wasn't always convenient.

The next time she arrived, the place was full of little boys dressed in super-hero cloaks, jumping off chairs they'd dragged into the back yard, or racing toy cars up and down the hallway.

'I'm a success at last!' said Martin, trying to be upbeat in the face of the woebegone expression on her face (*Not another bad day!*). 'Guess who was the lucky person chosen to look after all these kids while their mothers go off and have a girls' lunch?'

Emily stood there unresponsive, and when he next saw her she was lying on Pete's bed staring at the ceiling.

The children were always hungry. They clamoured for chocolate biscuits. 'Guys, guys!' Martin stood at the clothes-line, folding up towels. 'Just hang on a bit and I'll make you some proper lunch.' He went to where Emily still lay on Pete's bed and said, trying to keep the impatience from his voice, 'Do you think you could show the kids how to make some sandwiches?'

To his surprise, she got up and made her way to the kitchen, and actually organised them all with piles of sandwich ingredients. When they'd all eaten, she went back to the bed.

But after the children had finally been picked up (all at the same time, swept away by their mothers in a whirlwind of noise and confusion) he remembered her. She had actually been asleep in the midst of all that, but now she was awake, standing at the door of the living room looking as though she didn't know where she was.

Martin was slumped in a chair. 'Hey,' Pete bounced in. 'Remember that thing we got for Emmy?'

'What thing?'

'You know.'

'Oh, I know, the present.'

Pete ran into Martin's room and emerged with something wrapped in Christmas paper. He stopped, and threw it at Emily. 'Catch!'

'A present?'

'For Christmas!' yelled Pete.

'Pete . . . slow *down*.'

'Christmas?' said Emily. 'It isn't Christmas yet.'

'But we're going away,' said Martin. 'I told you. I'm sure I did. We're going to the coast to camp.'

'When are you going?'

'In about a week.'

'We're going to *swim* and *surf*, and . . . *swim*, and collect *shells* and it's going to be *fun!*' chanted Pete.

'Pete, not so *loud*.'

Pete ran over and started to pull the wrapping from Emily's present. It was a crocheted hat, like the one of Cat's that Emily used to wear, but purple, with a yellow flower on the side. Emily picked it up and held it. Not looking at the hat she said, panic-stricken, 'But I don't want you to *go*.'

'We haven't had a holiday for years,' said Martin, feeling put-upon. 'We're really looking forward to it, Emily – it's not often we get to go away.'

'Put it on,' urged Pete. He took the hat from her hands and jammed it on her head.

'Pete, just calm down a bit.' Martin leaned forward to look into her face. 'Emily,' he said, 'you'll be all *right*.'

Three

I

Emily walked, and mostly she noticed nothing. But one day a woman went past with a baby strapped to her front in a sling. The baby, whose head was still wobbly, used its arms to push back against its mother's chest; it looked up into her face and smiled. *Her* baby used to do just that. She was just about that age when Emily went away.

Mahalia.

She slept and woke with the cat on her chest. Had she dreamt of her baby? It was the first thing she thought of each morning – nothing as definite as *baby* or *Mahalia*, or a particular image; it was more that there was a continuing presence that didn't even need to be named.

One morning Charlotte came and sat beside her on the bed. In her hand she had something Emily had almost forgotten about: her logbook for learning to drive. 'Your father sent it,' said Charlotte. 'He says you were almost ready to get your licence; that you probably only need a few more lessons before taking the test.'

Emily took the booklet and flipped through the pages that recorded all the places and conditions she'd driven in. It seemed such a long time ago.

'Would you like to keep learning?'

'Okay,' said Emily, lying back against the pillow.

'Would you rather go to a driving school, or would you like me to take you out?'

'Would you?' said Emily.

'Of course. Do you have your permit with you?'

'I think so.' Emily took her wallet from the night table and looked inside. 'It's still here.'

'Great. When do you want to start? Today?'

'Would tomorrow be okay?' Emily lay back and closed her eyes. She wanted time to get used to the idea.

The next morning, Charlotte stood beside her bed with a cup of tea in her hand, and Emily reluctantly hauled herself out, though it wasn't early. It was painfully difficult to get dressed. Her grey tracksuit was cold and without comfort. More than anything, she would have liked to stay in bed and not think of a thing.

Emily tried to remember the routine. She checked that the mirrors were in position. She adjusted the seat, and put the key into the ignition.

Then she took off with the handbrake still on.

'Should have reminded you,' said Charlotte lightly.

'No. I *know* all this.'

Emily was used to her father's little old car, which smelt of leather and cracked varnish rather than brand-new plastic. She had begun driving when she was twelve. That was in the days when she was still happy to do things with her father. She remembered how he used to take her, illegally, on the dirt roads around her grandfather's farm, not so many years ago. She loved being behind the wheel. She felt that the whole world belonged to her. Once, there was nothing Emily couldn't do.

The thing about driving was, you needed to notice everything. The red car in front, the silver one behind. The woman with the stroller. The child in the flannelette shirt riding a bike and without a helmet. The old man with a stick. A border collie with a limp.

Who is here with us: Lots of people and animals I should try not to kill.

Emily's father used to push-start his old car sometimes. Run it down the hill and turn on the engine, hoping that it would catch.

Emily thought that if she could just push herself forward and pretend that she was operating okay, one day her engine would start up again.

2

Emily wanted to see Martin and Pete again before they went away. She knew that Martin had been losing patience with her. 'You'll be all *right*,' he'd said to her, and she wanted to show him that she would be.

She tried on the mauve hat with the yellow flower, turning this way and that in front of the mirror. She decided that she liked it, but what she liked most of all was that Martin and Pete had given it to her. She bought them something she hoped they'd like, chocolates that were shaped like sea shells, all different shapes.

As she wrapped the box she remembered the real shells she had collected once, which now probably lay scattered on the ground near the van in the country where she and Matt had lived for a while, just before and after the baby had been born.

Emily finished wrapping the chocolates and stood up, restlessly. Putting the present into her bag, she walked, first of all to the lookout because walking helped settle her feeling of agitation. Then she went quickly to Martin's place. The front door was shut, and she knocked, but there was no reply. Hearing a sound from the back yard, she went down the side of the house, calling out hello as she went.

Sleeping bags and towels festooned the clothesline, and a tent had been erected on the grass. Cat and Pete were crouched on the ground, rubbing away at something.

'Hello,' said Emily, and they looked up, so engrossed in what they were doing that they'd not noticed her.

'We're cleaning this!' said Pete, indicating some sort of tarpaulin that was covered with soapy water.

'Is Martin around?' said Emily.

'No, he's gone to do something,' said Cat. She looked up, and pushed hair out of her eyes with the back of her hand. She hadn't stood up to greet Emily, but squatted there barefoot, in shorts. There was sweat on her upper lip, making a beaded moustache.

Emily fingered the package that she'd stowed in her bag. She didn't know what to do, whether to wait, or leave the present, or go without leaving it.

'Can I help?' she said.

'Not really,' said Cat distractedly, making it clear that she found Emily's presence a bit of a trial. 'We're just trying to pack up to go away tomorrow.'

'You could get us a drink!' said Pete.

'Okay.' Emily dropped her bag onto the ground and went inside. Pete followed her, and they poured three glasses of juice and put them onto a tray, which Emily carried out. But in the yard, she stumbled, sending the glasses crashing onto the path.

'Oh . . .'

She heard Cat say, urgently, 'Pete, get away, you've got bare feet!'

'I'm sorry . . . Look, I'll . . .'

'No. I will, you've done enough. Pete, keep *away*!'

Emily blindly scrabbled at the broken glass, cramming it into her fist.

'Ow!' Blood welled from the palm of her hand. She dropped the glass she'd collected and staunched the blood with the bottom of her shirt.

'Mum! Emmy's hurt herself.'

'Oh! Now look what you've done.'

Emily closed her eyes and felt the thrill of the pain. She felt herself sway a little. For a moment there was only the blackness, and the pain in her hand. She opened her eyes and Cat and Pete were staring at her.

'Show me!' Cat reached out angrily to take hold of Emily's hand.

'No!'

She pulled away and held her hand defensively against her chest.

'Oh, don't be so stupid. Let me look.'

Emily backed away from her.

'Emmy, here's a teatowel.' Pete had run into the house and emerged brandishing a cloth. Emily took it and wrapped it round her hand. She noticed her bag lying on the ground. Not looking at either Pete or Cat, she picked it up and said, 'It'll be all right. Look, I'll just go now.'

She made her escape, walking the streets with her hand pressed into the teatowel. Passing a charity bin, she pulled the wrapped box of chocolates from her bag and pushed it into the slot.

'How did you do that, Emily?' asked Charlotte.

'I broke a glass.

'Round at Martin's place,' she added, though it hurt her to say his name.

Charlotte fetched iodine and sticking plaster, and Emily held out her hand obediently for it to be dressed.

'Are you too wounded for a driving lesson?' When Emily didn't reply, she said, 'Oh, go on! It's not that bad.'

The cut on Emily's hand throbbed as she drove up and down meaningless streets.

'Mind that dog!'

'I didn't see it.' Emily screeched the car to a halt, but the dog had already skipped sideways, narrowly avoiding her.

'Keep going,' said Charlotte quietly.

'It could have been a child,' said Emily. She found that her legs were shaking; she barely had the strength to press the accelerator.

In the mountains, the weather was ever changeable. It blew hot and cold, was brilliant sunshine in the morning, grew misty in the middle of the day, and squalled with rain in the evening. Clouds drifted across the sky in shifting patterns.

When she was awake she had to keep moving, her feet pounding down the footpaths. One foot in front of the other. No thinking. Streets led into streets. She walked into shops, and out again. People spoke to her and she fled.

'Girls are sharks.'

The man in the maroon jacket now wore a green T-shirt. He looked around, as though daring someone to challenge him. 'Girls are sharks.'

She saw him one day while she was out driving, had to

stop at a pedestrian crossing for him. She saw that he was silent that time, walking doggedly, staring at his feet, hands in pockets. She eased the car into movement, and she felt the power of it as it took off, sweeping down the street, leaving him behind. She watched the road, kept her eye on the mirrors, determined that nothing would surprise her again.

She walked to the edge of the town to her lookout, the one where she'd first seen Martin standing outside the safety fence. She thought how the town perched above the valley precipitously, too close to the sky and too far from the sea. She saw the yellow flowers gripping onto the rocks. She went past Martin's place, but the front door was closed and the place looked abandoned. They had gone away. A child's sneaker lay on the veranda upside down. She walked on. Flocks of black cockatoos screeched through the sky and landed heavily in the pine trees, making the branches shudder.

Emily found herself one day at the shops. They were full of Christmas things – wrapping paper and packaged mince pies and fruitcakes. Images of Santa were everywhere. She thought of her baby. She thought of Mahalia.

At the ATM she withdrew a small amount of money. To her astonishment, when she checked the slip, she had over three hundred dollars left in the account. She remembered Charlotte saying that her parents were giving her a small allowance. She hadn't wanted their money, and hadn't looked in her account for ages.

In a chainstore she flicked through racks of babies' clothes: impossibly small jumpsuits covered with teddy bears or plain ones in pink, yellow, blue or white. Then there were slightly larger clothes in brighter colours – dark blue and red, or bright green. And bigger clothes still – little sundresses with ruffled hems, or baby-sized cargo pants. A feeling of panic gripped her, and she wiped a tear from her eye as she pushed her way out of the shop. She had absolutely no idea what size her baby would be now, or what would be suitable to get her. She didn't even know of a way to even begin imagining it.

In a toyshop, she looked at blocks and musical trains and various dolls and toy animals and remote-control cars, and every-thing seemed increasingly unreal to her. What should she buy? Anything was suitable. Nothing was. Again, she walked out.

She was in an enclosed shopping centre and the walkways were crowded and confused. Voices and music assaulted her on all sides. Above it all she heard the high, piping sound of a bird. She thought at first that it was a part of the recorded music, but when she looked up she saw a sparrow perched on one of the lights. She watched as it took off, streaking swiftly under the ceiling, looking for a way out. Unsuccessful, it returned the way it had come, and sat on top of the light again.

Emily made her way to the toilets, where she sat hunched in a cubicle, staring at her feet. She tore a piece of toilet paper from the roll and used it to mop her eyes and blow her nose. The rough paper scratched her skin, and she searched in her pockets for a tissue, but found none.

She flushed the toilet and emerged to wash her hands. Wadded-up tissue paper clogged the basin, and swirled dismally as she ran the tap. 'I hate you!' yelled a child from one of the cubicles. 'I hate you and I want my mum! I'll tell her how you smacked me.' Emily leaned against the basin and took a deep breath. She wiped her hands quickly on her pants and pushed her way through the door.

Out on the walkway again, she heard the plaintive sound of the bird, high above the voices and music. Emily felt dizzy. She looked for a way out.

She felt lost and helpless. Apart from not being able to picture her baby, she realised that she didn't even know what day of the week it was – or what month. She tried to think of what town she was in, and again drew a blank. It was as though she had lost a part of her mind. She existed in a world where time and place meant nothing. And she was nothing.

She stumbled through the shopping centre until finally she came to a huge plate-glass door that opened wide as she approached. She made her escape, and her feet took her back to Charlotte's place.

There she crawled into bed. It was a warm day, but Emily pulled the cover up over her head, and kept her hands up sheltering the front of her face, and cried.

She heard the back door slam, and Charlotte moving around in the kitchen. Then she sensed someone at the door of the room.

'Emily?'

The side of the mattress dipped.

'Emily . . . are you in there?'

Emily sniffed the tears into the back of her throat.

A hand reached out and pulled the cover gently away from her face. Emily turned.

'Hey, what's the matter?'

'I'm having a really bad day . . .'

And then it all came out – about not knowing what to buy the baby for Christmas because of not knowing how big she'd be, down to the way her mind had even lost the basic knowledge of what day it was.

'And do you think you know what day it is now?'

Emily swallowed some mucus. 'Tuesday?' she asked apprehensively.

Charlotte smiled. 'Correct. Come out to the kitchen and I'll get you a drink.'

When Emily sat huddled at the table with a glass of apple juice in front of her, Charlotte said, gently, 'Emily, you need help.'

'Do you think I need to see a doctor?'

'Probably. To tell you the truth, I feel so helpless with you sometimes. But you know what? A present for Mahalia, that I could help with.'

Together they sat there at the table and figured out what

Mahalia would like for Christmas. 'My children always loved toy animals,' said Charlotte. 'She's about eleven months now, so she'll be picking up things and holding them. She'll be noticing animals, finding them quite exciting – real ones, that is – to touch, and pat. So a toy animal would go down really well.'

Emily looked past Charlotte's shoulder, and thought about it. The exact perfect present came to her. 'A horse,' she said, nodding decisively. 'I'll get her a toy horse.'

A moment later she said, 'Can we take the car down to the shops now to get it? I can drive.'

Emily lay under a lemon tree in Charlotte's back yard. Charlotte was out, visiting one of her friends. Earlier on, she'd made a cake to take with her, and had left the bowl in the kitchen for Emily to lick. She seemed to think that Emily might enjoy this; Charlotte sometimes treated her like a child, Emily thought, and so she'd stubbornly left the bowl untouched. Instead, she'd gone out to lie in the back yard under the tree, where her vision was full of leaves and flowers and yellow fruit, and her hearing full of the sound of bees.

She'd bought a plush horse for Mahalia, silky smooth to pat like a real horse, and wrapped it in Christmas paper and sent it in a padded envelope. She'd not known what to write on the card; she knew that a horse was inadequate, that what the baby needed was her, and in the end she'd scrawled a hasty note, *Thinking of you both heaps*, which was intended for Matt as well, because she still didn't know what to write to him. The problem of Matt was something else altogether.

Emily closed her eyes and felt something like content-ment. For now, there was the scent of lemon and the bees. When her head was almost bursting with it all, she got to her feet and went to the kitchen where dreamily she licked out the bowl of chocolate mixture with her finger. She was so full of the scent of lemon blossom she imagined it must seep out from her skin. Alone in the house, she wandered about, feeling insubstantial, merely a scent, a shadow of the lemony essence of the tree.

The house was so full of Charlotte's *stuff*, and so quiet, the cat sleeping weightily on the sofa, and the angel in a green dress with a posy of flowers, and the lovers forever levitating in the ecstasy of love.

The phone rang. Wanting to stop the sound that jangled through the house, she picked it up.

'Hello? Hello? Is that you, Emily?'

And again. 'Hello. Emily? This is Mum . . .'

Emily opened her mouth like a fish, and a bubble of lemon-scented air emerged, but nothing else. She walked backwards a few steps, as if to get away, but holding out the cordless receiver in front of her at arm's length. She could hear a small voice coming from it. It sounded like one of the small buzzing insects that sometimes became trapped in bottles, or built nests behind the paintings. Cautiously, Emily put the receiver to her ear.

The voice on the other end had ceased, but the line was still open. 'Hello,' she whispered.

'Hello?' came her mother's voice, softly. 'Emily?'

'Yes.'

'How are you?'

'I'm – I'm okay.'

Both of them were speaking so softly, it was almost as if the conversation was not taking place.

'It's good to speak to you. What are you doing today?'

'Oh, nothing much. I'm afraid Charlotte's not here.'

'That's all right. I wanted to speak to you.'

Emily could think of nothing to say.

'Emily?'

'Yes.'

'I've sent you a package for Christmas – a few things I thought you might like. Some clothes – I hope you don't mind me choosing them – the girl at the shop was only a bit older than you and I took her advice.'

'No, that's all right – I mean, thanks.'

'I was wondering if you'd had any thoughts about coming home.'

Emily remained silent.

'It's just that – you know, if you wanted, you could live here with us, with Mahalia.'

'I don't know. I hadn't thought . . .'

'Well, think about it. Mahalia's been visiting us on her own – staying the night. She's a lovely little thing.'

Emily was silent. she imagined her baby staying with her mother.

'I have to go now,' she said abruptly.

'Oh – all right then. Bye, darling. I'll ring again.'

Emily put the receiver back onto the cradle.

She put her face in her hands, but no tears came. Retreating to her bed, she curled up on top of the cover. The cat came inquiringly into the room and jumped up onto her, but she pushed it away, and started to pick at a join in the wallpaper. She didn't want to think, and somehow the picking helped. It was slow work, for the paper was glued on tight. She had picked away a patch the size of a fifty-cent coin by the time she noticed that the cut in her hand had somehow opened up again. She squeezed it till it bled.

'Emily?'

She hadn't heard Charlotte come home.

'Having a nap?'

Emily hauled herself up with difficulty. 'Just a lie-down,' she said.

She followed Charlotte out to the kitchen, still feeling dis-oriented. 'Did you have a nice . . . chocolate cake?' she asked feebly.

Charlotte patted her on the arm. 'I see you licked the bowl, then. Do you feel like a driving lesson? You're going so well, it'd be a shame not to keep up the momentum.'

Emily looked around. 'Don't you want . . . a cup of tea

first?' she said, hoping to put it off. She had no energy for driving today. She rarely had the energy for driving.

'I'm stuffed to the gills with tea,' said Charlotte. Instead of dropping the car keys onto the bench, she said, 'Catch.'

To her own astonishment, Emily caught them.

6

(A postcard with a picture of dolphins)

Dear Emily,

Well, we're here at the coast at last, and it's everything the beach should be: sunny, with cool, perfect water. Pete's having a great time swimming every day, and there's an icecream shop almost next door to the camping ground, so he's set.

Sorry to have missed you the day you called round. Hope to see you when we get back. Have a lovely Christmas.

Love, Martin and Pete

PS We <u>did</u> see some dolphins. One jumped out of the water only about 50 metres in front of us!

7

Sometimes, when she woke, she imagined herself at her parents' house, even though she'd lived in several places since she'd left it. She imagined that the light coming through the window was the light of a North Coast summer, and outside, her father would be tinkering with his old car. Dressed in his shabby weekend pants, he'd be leaning into the bonnet, polishing the engine and pulling out the oil gauge to view it critically and wipe it clean.

Her mother . . .

Emily forced her eyes properly open and saw the wall where she'd been picking away the wallpaper. It was now a patch the size of an orange. The house was quiet. In the doorway, the cat sat staring at her.

Emily remembered Charlotte leaving before sunrise to drive to the station. She was catching the train down to the city for the day to have Christmas with her family. Emily had been firm about not wanting to go with her; she had put on a show of normality the day before, getting up early and sitting down to breakfast, and later on eating two slices of Christmas cake. She swore to Charlotte that she'd be all right on her own. 'It's no big deal, is it? It's just a day.' Finally she'd resorted to saying callously, 'Anyway, I'd be *so* bored down there with them all.'

Charlotte had tiptoed into the room earlier in the half-dark and put something on the end of her bed. Now, stretching her toe to feel for it, Emily made the object fall onto the floor.

They'd already exchanged presents the night before, so this was extra. Emily was still wearing the glass bead necklace that Charlotte had given her. Now she peeled away the tape and out tumbled some bath bombs and two cakes of soap that looked and smelt like something to eat.

In the kitchen, she looked at the clock. It was eleven-thirty. This time last year she and Matt had been at his mother Julie's place, high on a mountain surrounded by forest. Emily had sighed a lot in the heat, putting her hand on her belly to feel the baby kick and turn over. There'd been an assortment of people there: some friends of Julie's, and a few stray people she'd felt sorry for. It was sad, she said, to have to spend Christmas on your own.

That was probably where Matt and the baby were now. While Emily stood in a deathly quiet kitchen in the Blue Mountains, her baby would be sitting on a verandah surrounded by wrapping paper, or crawling around under the feet of people Emily had never met. The sky would be a brilliant blue, but clouds would be already gathering for an afternoon storm.

The fridge door creaked as she opened it. Charlotte had left a large festive platter of meats and salads, and a plum pudding she'd told Emily she could have with icecream. Peeling up the corner of the plastic covering, Emily extracted a slice of cold ham, folded it, and put it into her mouth. She gave a slice to the cat, and ate some potato salad with her fingers.

She ran a deep bath and immersed herself, lying on her back with her hair floating around her. She thought she heard the phone ringing; sitting up, she listened until it stopped, then ran more water into the bath.

A wave of water sloshed over the edge when she hauled herself out. She left the deluge on the floor and towelled herself dry. With her hair dripping down her back, she trailed around the house naked. She wondered if other people felt like this – as though they weren't quite real. The light on the answering machine blinked, but she ignored it.

Wrapping a sarong around her, she sat for a long time under the tree in the back yard. Finally, mid-afternoon, she went inside and dressed in the clothes that her mother had sent her. She almost smiled at herself in the full-length mirror in Charlotte's room, where she'd gone to see how she looked. She was surprised that she still looked okay – just like any other girl in the short, layered skirt and lacy halter-neck top.

She was all dressed up with nowhere to go. She moved a pile of art books and sat down on one of Charlotte's many sofas, staring up at the angel in the green dress, who looked mysterious in the shadowy afternoon light. Late afternoons were the worst, just before nightfall. She'd often been around at Martin's place at that time, watching Pete while he had his bath, or cooking with Martin in the kitchen before Cat came home from work. It had helped her, to be absorbed by something at the wolfish time of day that threatened to eat you up with its loneliness.

Emily had felt detached and removed from the world in the weeks before her baby was born. She and Matt had moved to a caravan in the hills outside the town, and she'd delighted in everything she found there at first – the way the clouds changed shape continually, the starry nights when they lay outside on the grass talking and staring at the sky, the rocky creek at the bottom of the hill where they swam naked, and the big old tree under which they lay for hours afterwards on the hottest of days.

Then Emily found all her energy becoming concentrated somehow inside herself – she felt she must be giving it all to the baby. When Matt spoke to her, she found herself responding from a long way away. She wasn't with him, not really.

It was vaguely pleasant, this remoteness. She knew that she was storing herself up, gathering herself together, for the big thing that she would have to do.

Emily had imagined their baby being born somewhere spacious and beautiful and calm, perhaps under the spreading fig tree in the paddock where she and Matt lay after swimming in the creek. She'd wanted something magical and otherworldly.

The labour room in the hospital was far from her fantasy,

even though there was a forest scene on the wall, and the nurses played music that was meant to be soothing. None of it helped. Emily had disappeared inside a small burning circle of pain.

When she emerged, she was not the same person, and she had a child. The tiny creature had slipped from her in a rush, so that she felt it must be a seal, not a human being.

Matt had loved the baby at once, unable to take his eyes away, marvelling at her fingers and toes and her perfect little face. His enthusiasm had made Emily smile, but already she was beginning to be afraid.

She wanted, more than anything, for her mother to come and tell her that everything would be all right.

Once, she'd contained this baby inside her. Now, the child seemed contained within herself. She must have been that way all along, floating inside Emily with that self-possessed set to her mouth, her eyes tightly closed and inward-looking.

The baby lay in its crib beside her bed, and Emily had rolled over to face the wall, so she didn't have to look at it. The baby was self-possessed, yet helpless, and Emily wondered how she – weak, imperfect, headstrong Emily – could ever give her everything she would need.

Matt's mother Julie came, and stood beside the crib gazing into the baby's face with tears in her eyes. 'She is so beautiful – just so beautiful.' She reached out one tentative finger to touch the baby's sleeping face. She'd brought armfuls of flowers from her garden, and so many presents that Emily felt overwhelmed. She was still a little in awe of Julie, who had raised Matt all on her own, and built her house with her own two hands, and had a job as a social worker.

Emily had waited for her own mother, and waited.

9

Emily got up and wandered restlessly around Charlotte's house. She opened the refrigerator and stared into it, but she wasn't hungry. While she was prowling about, the phone started to ring, and she stood nearby and watched it until the answering machine cut in.

'Hello, Emily, this is Dad. Just ringing to wish you – and Charlotte of course – a happy Christmas. Mum rang earlier and left a message, but I suppose you were both out – and still are . . .'

Her father's voice faltered. He wasn't used to giving messages to machines.

'Anyway, love, I hope you're having a nice day. Give us a ring when you get back? Bye for now.'

The machine clicked off. Emily, who'd been almost ready to reach out and pick up the receiver, turned and walked out of the house.

10

When her mother had finally come to the hospital, she'd glanced at the baby in the cradle almost in embarrassment, and planted a dutiful kiss on Emily's cheek. Then she stood awkwardly, holding a bunch of flowers and a present that Emily didn't unwrap until long after she'd left.

For a long time she and Emily had not got along; Emily felt that her mother too often tried to tell her what to do, while at other times she seemed a little afraid. Emily had reacted to both these approaches with a dismissive sigh.

Her father had been more welcoming. 'Hello, Emmy, my darling?' peering anxiously around the door before he came in, as though afraid of surprising her in some unspeakable medical procedure. He held her close for a long time.

'So this is the little one.' He turned back the edge of the baby blanket, and said coyly, 'May I?' before picking her up and cradling her in her arms. 'Oh, look, Margaret,' he said. 'Our first grandchild.'

Emily's mother allowed the baby to be thrust into her arms; Emily saw her soften slightly, before returning the child to her husband.

'What is the babe's name?' he asked shyly.

'Mahalia,' she said.

He didn't quite understand, and she had to repeat it.

'Mahalia,' he said. 'That's . . . unusual, isn't it? But I like it, I think,' he said warmly, turning to his wife, who nodded, curtly.

Emily remembered the way her parents had always made her feel hemmed in. Her childhood dream of horses had been a way of escape from them. A horse had strength, and swiftness, and unpredictability. You could be free on a horse. She'd written a story when she was in primary school about running away on her imaginary horse. In the story she'd gone as far as Western Australia, and when she saw headlines in the paper that her parents were looking for her she hadn't felt one bit of remorse.

When she was too young to know what she was doing they'd stuck her in a white dress and taken her to the church and had her confirmed in a faith that she could never take seriously. Years later, she had coaxed the priest into allowing her to climb up the church tower. And she'd taken Matt with her, pulling him up the dim stone staircase, and kissed him for the first time right on top of the tower. She hoped that everyone would see them, but feared that no one had.

And she'd jumped into the river one day, just to see what it felt like. It had been cold and muddy and exhilarating. She'd wanted to shock herself awake, to experience everything. She'd wanted more than the pretty pink bedroom in her parents' house.

Lying in the hospital bed with her baby beside her, she could see that not only had she hemmed herself in again, she'd also thoughtlessly implicated a child who hadn't asked for life at all.

11

As Emily walked away from Charlotte's house, there were very few people about, and the streets had the weary flatness that she remembered from other Christmas afternoons. She walked past Martin's house through habit. One of Pete's sneakers still lay sole up on the front verandah in exactly the same position it had been in last time.

In the town centre she went into a milk bar and stood waiting to be served. The girl behind the counter was wiping down the stainless steel with a thick grey rag; it swirled around, leaving beads of water on the gleaming surface. Three people about Emily's age sat at a booth in the dim recesses of the café. She heard a boy's voice say, 'Hey! She's hot!' and a girl's derisive laugh. Finally the shop assistant came up to her with an expression that implied she was being interrupted, and Emily asked politely for a chocolate milkshake.

She glanced towards the back of the shop to the faces in the booth; she noticed only a girl with a plump, freckled face who looked away from her and down into her milkshake with a smirk.

As the shopgirl dipped a ladle into the refrigerator to scoop up the milk, Emily realised that she had come out without her bag. 'I'm sorry,' she interrupted her, 'I'll have to cancel that – I've forgotten my purse,' and fled without looking back.

She found a park and squirted water into her mouth from a bubbler. The place had an air of desertion, and because of the welcome lack of people Emily sat down on a seat. She didn't want to go back to Charlotte's place yet. It would feel at once too constricting and too empty. The light on the answering machine would blink insistently at her. Her parents could even ring again, and she mightn't be able to resist answering.

An Indian family – people of all ages, including a couple of toddlers – came into the park and spread out picnic rugs. They carried several pots wrapped in teatowels, and picnic baskets. The oldest woman unwrapped the pots and ladled rice and curry onto plates. Another poured steaming tea from a thermos and handed the cups round. The children were given soft drink. The men sat to one side of the picnic rugs and talked and smoked.

Then they ate, laughing and talking all the while, and the toddlers staggered about and collapsed onto their bottoms on the ground when their legs gave way. Whenever one came within their orbit, one or other of the women would press rice into its willing mouth with her fingers.

Emily saw a single figure enter the path at the far side of the park. She knew from the rangy look of him, the bare feet and the matted hair, that it was the lonely boy whose eyes Martin had noticed were so blue. He walked along the path until he came level with the Indian family, stopped and stared at them for a moment, and then walked on with his steady, purposeless trudge. The family did not notice him (as indeed they had not noticed Emily), and Emily wondered if the lonely boy had been there at all, or if she'd imagined it. And she wondered if she was there either, she seemed so nebulous, the world swirling around her as if nothing existed at all, least of all Emily herself.

12

The caravan where they'd lived was high in the hills, and had views of the surrounding countryside; it was like living in an eagle's nest.

There they had lived in a sort of idyllic dream – had cooked outside on a campfire, and lain under the stars at night when the van became too hot. When Emily and the baby came out of hospital they returned there – both insisted on it, though Matt's mother had wanted them to come and stay with her for a while.

The place, which to Emily had previously felt like paradise, was now too bleak and uncomfortable. They shared a bath with Kevin, the man who owned the property – it was an old enamel tub in the open, attached to the back of his house. Nappies had to be washed by hand in Kevin's laundry tub, also in the open air. Everything was a struggle. Emily felt that they were too exposed to the elements. The sun was too hot and relentless, the wind too windy, the nights black.

Matt had been eager to do as much as he could to help. He did all the washing and cooking. He woke the moment the baby cried at night, and gave her to Emily to feed. But she found breastfeeding difficult. The baby hunted for the nipple so frantically, moving her head rapidly from side to side, it was as though she was really fighting to get away from it. And then she'd cry, and Emily would cry. By the time the baby managed to latch on to feed they were both exhausted.

They spent a week living in the van. In that time, Emily felt that they were isolated and alone. Perched up there above the world didn't feel like paradise. It felt like exile. She was alone with the baby in a hostile, unforgiving world.

It had been a relief to stay with Matt's mother. Julie had come to visit, saw at once how impossible it was with a baby, and insisted they come to live with her.

Her place was on the side of a mountain covered with rainforest; the only sounds were the cries of whipbirds, or the soft booming coo of native pigeons.

They had a whole huge bedroom and the use of the rest of the house. There was a washing machine and a proper kitchen; things that Emily had once taken for granted. When she'd first met Matt, she'd thought the place where he lived was strange after the suburban brick house she'd been raised in, because it had been built out of second-hand materials, but it had all the comforts you needed.

The house had a wonderful bathroom with bright, hand-made tiles. Emily would lie in the bath and look out a door and see bush, and sky. Most of the time they spent there was bliss. Matt was a most attentive father; he picked up the baby when she stirred at night and brought her to Emily, and the look on his face when he gazed at both of them made Emily feel cherished.

But her parents never visited. Her mother knew that Matt lived far out in the hills in what some people in town called a *hippy house*, and it was the sort of place her mother would never set foot in. Even though Julie offered to take her and the baby into town to visit *them*, Emily was too proud. And she was happy up there in that house; she didn't feel the need to go anywhere.

It was Matt who'd wanted to move into a place on their own. 'We can't live with my mum forever,' he said.

And so they moved into town, to the flat at the back of an old house, into what Emily later thought of as the white room.

The room was very white. It was an enclosed verandah, and had a length of frosted glass windows along the front. In the morning it was so bright it was like being in the glare of a spotlight. And in the afternoon, when the sun shifted away, the room shaded into near-darkness, speaking to her of loss and loneliness.

She spent almost five months in that room. At one end was a small kitchen; at the other a shabby bathroom. The laundry they shared with the old woman whose house it was in – it was under the house, and had an unsavoury odour of damp soil.

Emily rarely went out; she let Matt do all the shopping. Her few friends had drifted away. If she did go out, there was the sense of everything being different. There seemed to be no skin, no protection between her and the rest of the world. She felt no connection with anything.

There was only a profound sense of loss. She would lie for hours and listen to Matt play softly on his guitar. The baby would at least grow up with music. *Blues is the music that heals*, he'd lettered on the side of his guitar case. She wondered if the music might heal her. It was a bass guitar, its notes low and thrumming, its rhythm like a heartbeat.

'Are you okay?' Matt would ask, nestling down next to her on the bed where she spent nearly the whole of each day.

'Me? I'm fine,' she'd tell him. He seemed to believe it, and she longed for him to say something to indicate that he knew she wasn't all right at all.

She'd hear the locks of the guitar case click shut. *Snap. Snap.* Matt would pick up his guitar and escape, off to jam with his friend Otis.

Her father came to visit, by himself. He seemed to enjoy sitting on the sofa with the baby on his lap, a cup of tea going cold on the floor beside him. After that, he often popped in to see them on his way to golf, or meetings of his car club. Emily felt sure her mother knew nothing of these visits.

Then one day she was there at the door beside him.

She came into the kitchen and stood while Emily made them cups of tea. Emily was able to remember that they both took milk. She removed the teabags, searched for a saucer to deposit them on and settled for the edge of the sink, where they sat leaking mud-coloured liquid. Emily's mother looked around. 'I wanted more for you than this,' was all she said.

The baby was asleep that day in a basket in the living room, and they sat around her and talked softly and awkwardly. The baby was often asleep; she was a good baby. Emily had been astonished by the strength of her purity and calmness. It scared her, the responsibility of looking after such a precious creature.

Emily's father peeped into the basket and turned back the edge of the blanket. 'They say you should never wake a sleeping baby,' he said softly, with an impish twinkle, 'but it's hard to resist, isn't it?'

That day Emily, too, wished the baby wasn't asleep – it might give them something to look at and talk about. But she didn't wake, and Emily's parents left after a while. She felt for a long time the cool kiss her mother gave her on departing.

Emily found that she was good at pretending. She could get dressed up when she had to, and go out, and pretend cheerfulness and competency. 'Yeah, in the end I decided that I couldn't be bothered with breastfeeding,' she said to Matt's mother, on a visit to her place one day. 'With a bottle, Matt can feed her, and I don't have to worry about having enough milk.'

She energetically chopped fruit for a fruit salad, tossing pineapple skin into a pile. She laughed (she could still laugh!). 'I'm thinking of taking up belly-dancing!' she lied. 'Can't do that with boobs full of milk.'

Matt's mother looked at her with concern, and later asked her, 'Are you sure you're coping okay? I mean, it's all right not to, you know.'

'God, yes,' said Emily. 'I mean, she's so good – haven't you noticed? And Matt does heaps.'

Emily called it her *big front*, the way she was able to fool people. She felt that nothing was real any more. And above all, she was not real.

She worried that something would happen to the baby. There was so much that could go wrong. Car crashes, house fires, drowning. She feared her child would get caught up in some disaster, if not now, then at some later time in her life. Or she could simply die in her sleep – some babies did – or become ill. Emily felt helpless in the face of all these imagined catastrophes. She was inadequate, a *bad mother*.

She cared for Mahalia mechanically. She changed nappies, wiped pink goo onto her bottom, made up bottles, in ceaseless repetition. Nothing gave her any joy. Always, there was the knowledge that she'd wanted more for her baby than she was capable of giving her.

Then she became afraid that it was she who would do harm to the baby. She put all the knives in a drawer and tried to pretend they weren't there. She threw Matt's Stanley knife, which had such a tempting deep, sharp blade, into the bin and then retrieved it and hid it under the sink cupboard.

She first cut herself on the arm one day when Matt was out taking the baby for a walk. Alone in the house, she felt drawn to the cupboard where she'd hidden the Stanley knife. In the dim afternoon light in the kitchen it looked so harmless at first, with its red plastic handle and short, sloping blade. Staring wonderingly at the knife, she felt that nothing she did would matter. She wondered whether any action she performed would have a real, tangible result.

The first cut had been the most difficult, and the most thrilling. It had taken ages for her to steel herself into drawing the blade across the pale skin of her inner arm, just heavy enough to make a fine cut a few centimetres long. The sting of it had exhilarated her, and she'd stared at the thread of blood that had appeared. When it began to spill into drops she took a wad of tissue and mopped it up, her heart beating rapidly, afraid that she might have cut too deep.

By the time Matt came home she was on the bed, feigning sleep. He was used to her sleeping in the afternoons, and excused it because everyone knew that babies tired you out.

Afterwards, on other days, she cut herself again. It was winter, and she was able to cover her arms with long sleeves, and managed to conceal the marks on her arms from Matt.

Each time she gave in to temptation and damaged herself again she hated herself even more.

Finally, in August, after days of wind had buffeted the house so relentlessly she thought she would scream, she decided that she would go. Matt and the baby would be better off without her. Matt did most of the care of the baby anyway. He did it with love, smiling and talking to her and looking into her face with adoration. And the baby smiled back at him, squirming her body with pleasure. The closest Emily came to happiness was when she saw them together.

She packed her bag when Matt was out one afternoon. She'd already rung Charlotte and asked if she could stay with her.

It was better if it was done quickly.

Matt looked shattered when she told him that she was going. But he walked her to the bus station, holding the baby in a sling on his front. She tried not to think of the expression on his face as the bus pulled away.

13

The Indian family were packing up their picnic. It was almost nightfall. Emily watched them depart, lugging their baskets and empty pots, the women reaching out for the hands of the children, the men smoothing back the sides of their hair and dusting off the seats of their pants. A lingering child zipped down the slippery slide one last time and ran to catch up with the others.

A figure appeared through the trees. It was a silhouette, lit up round the edges from the rays of the setting sun and dark in the middle. As it got closer Emily thought it looked like the man she thought of as the shark man, but she didn't take much notice. The figure seemed to hover, uncertain, hands in pockets, and then veered off to one side, only to reappear a little later. She saw him pause and regard her, rather like a dog unsure of its welcome, and then he disappeared from her line of vision as she was staring steadfastly ahead, refusing to acknowledge his presence.

She only noticed him again when he landed like a large, clumsy bird on the end of the seat she was on, making the wooden slats shiver with his weight. She didn't want to get up and go straight away; she would rather not have to react to him. She thought he might just leave anyway.

And then he was right next to her, having slid somehow along the seat. He sighed, a soft, resigned sound. She caught his odour, which was sweetish and sickly, rather like musk sticks.

His hand, heavy and meaty, fell on her thigh, as though by accident. All this time he had said nothing, and Emily had not looked directly at him. She had a feeling of disbelief; that she must be imagining it.

In one swift movement she got to her feet and flung his hand from her leg. She stood rigidly, unsure of what to do next, holding up her hands stiffly next to her shoulders in a gesture that said, *Enough!*

And still without looking at him she walked steadily away, out of the park, and up the suburban street, where there were at least signs of life and safety. Occasional families were arriving home in cars from which fractious children were emerging with arms laden with gifts.

Emily had no idea where she was going; she just walked, aware that he was following her some way behind.

14

When Emily had boarded the bus the night she left Matt and the baby, she'd shut all thought from her mind. She couldn't afford to think, or to feel.

She found a spare seat halfway along the bus and shoved her shoulder bag into the overhead locker. It was nightfall and the tinted glass in the window was close to black. Emily stared through the window. There was a blur that might have been Matt's face, and then thankfully the doors swung shut and the bus slid out of the station. She retreated to a place inside herself, aware only of the glare of the overhead lights and the irritating beat of old pop songs on the driver's radio.

There was a woman sitting next to her. 'You going far?' she asked Emily.

'Yes. Sydney.'

'All the way! Holiday?'

'Yes.'

'I'm going down to my daughter. Just as far as Coffs.'

Emily smiled politely and stared out the window. Then she got up and pulled a fleecy jacket from her bag, folded it, and put it against the glass and pretended to sleep. She did fall asleep, for when she next came to, the woman who'd been sitting beside her had gone.

It was a long night. Emily shuffled off the bus at various stops, splashing her face with water in anonymous rest rooms and bowing her head in front of the mirror so that she wouldn't be confronted with her own face. She preferred to imagine that she didn't exist, that this wasn't happening to her. In the bright glare of a fast-food outlet she unexpectedly caught sight of herself reflected in a plate-glass window and was shocked by how *okay* she looked. She had to look again to make sure that it was actually herself, and not some other curly-haired, short-skirted girl.

There was a boy watching her. She saw him as she moved away from the window. He was dressed in jeans and a hooded top, and had the hollow-cheeked gaze of someone perpetually hungry. He devoured a hamburger with absent-minded ferocity; when he'd finished he screwed up the paper and shoved it in the bin.

Emily returned to the bus and as she sat down noticed him coming up the aisle. He disappeared into a seat further up. After the bus pulled out, someone plonked down into the empty aisle seat beside her. He sighed, and said, 'What's your name?'

Emily's body stiffened. She didn't reply, ignoring him, hoping he'd go away. He said nothing more, just settled in and sat beside her in the darkened bus as it rushed through the night, occasional car lights appearing like searchlights and illuminating their faces.

After a while the boy sighed again and settled down as if to sleep, his head falling onto her shoulder as though by accident. She pushed it gently away, but it fell sideways again.

With the weight of his head against her shoulder, Emily wondered what to do. She couldn't bear the thought of having to do anything – of confronting him, making a fuss, risking some kind of scene, having the lights come on, being the centre of attention. She sat dully and stared out of the black window. The boy started to snore, lightly and evenly. He smelt of sweat and cigarette smoke and fried onions. When she leaned her head against the window and closed her eyes he settled more solidly against her, sliding over to accommodate her new position.

He reached out and took her hand.

And Emily let him hold it. It was a soft, trusting, needy hand, and she found it strangely comforting. She left him like that, with his hand in hers. She didn't know if she was comforting him, or if he was comforting her. Perhaps they were comforting each other. Resting her head against the shuddering windowpane, she closed her eyes.

She woke at dawn and he was gone. She sat up and adjusted her clothes, as though people were watching her. And then they reached the city, where Charlotte stood

waiting to take her to her daughter's place for breakfast and a
shower before going up to the mountains.

Emily walked through the streets with the shark man following at a distance. She turned and caught a glimpse of him
from time to time.

She rounded a corner and a church reared up in front of
her. It was as imposing as only a Catholic cathedral can be.
Cars were parked all about it, in the street and car park. A few
latecomers hurried through the doors, clutching the hands of
their children.

Christmas Day Mass.

Emily stood in front of the building and stared up. Behind
it the sky was navy blue – not quite dark yet. Emily took a
breath, and exhaled. She had not been inside this particular
building but she knew exactly what she would find inside.

It would be all light and dark. Pools of light and the
candles throwing shadows. The brown polished wood.
Splashes of colour like jewels. Everything shiny and burn-
ished – the people too. Children slicked down with comb
marks in their hair, dressed in their best. She saw it all: the
shuffling, the rustle of hymn books, the discreet throat-
clearing, the music swelling and receding, the scuffle of
people kneeling for prayer. The sign of the cross. There would

be teenagers smirking, surreptitiously making fun of the proceedings, secretly disbelieving.

And it occurred to her that she could walk right in and be a part of it. She could belong. She could go into the church, stand in line for communion, shuffle forward, put out her tongue and swallow. She could steal into the intimacy of the confessional. She could do it all.

For a moment she wanted to. She wanted to find the child she once was, the girl in the white frock with scratchy lace, and the pure white never-before-worn socks and the shiny black court shoes. If she could go back to *then* and start it all again . . .

But starting again wasn't possible. She wasn't even sure she did want things to be different. She didn't want to regret anything.

She walked quickly away down the street the way she had come. Stopping in front of the shark man she said to him loudly, 'If you keep following me I'll call the police.'

She walked back to Charlotte's place. The car was back in the drive, and the lights were on in the house.

Emily quickened her step. 'I'm home!' she called, as she let herself in.

Four

I

Emily cannot tell where the process of getting better started. Perhaps it was the day she felt trapped in the shopping centre, the day Charlotte helped her buy the toy horse for Mahalia. Or it may have begun further back, when she met Martin and Pete, and slowly started to feel part of life again. Or when Charlotte came into her room with the logbook that her father had posted up to her. Or the evening she stopped in front of the shark man and told him to stop following her.

It doesn't matter. All that does is that a veil no longer shrouds her. The world is clearer, colours brighter. She has a sense of possibilities again. Somehow, the world seems to have shifted to accommodate her.

Or she to it.

She has space inside her. Her blood beats surely in her veins. Her breath comes slowly and easily.

The cat knows she is different. In the mornings it butts its head into her hand and purrs.

She has started to eat breakfast at a regular, reasonably

early hour. At night in bed she runs her hands over her ribs. They don't stick out so much now.

If I don't watch it I'll get fat!

But she asks for seconds of dessert every night.

She pesters Charlotte to take her driving.

'Not again!'

Charlotte laughs, as Emily grabs the keys and heads outside. She loves Charlotte's little yellow car: it's as bright and as shiny as a jellybean. The magnetic L-plates attach with a soft kissing sound. And it does everything she wants it to do.

She makes Charlotte take her out in the worst weather: in torrential rain, and late at night. 'You need to get used to all kinds of conditions,' she tells her. 'That's what Dad used to say.'

On fine evenings she walks around the streets, catching the scent of flowers, savouring the night. She glances through lighted windows, and hears snatches of the lives within, no longer feeling apart from it all.

She walks past Martin and Pete's house, still closed-up and dark, not expecting them to be at home. Earlier in the day she noticed that the sneaker still lay untouched in the same position on the verandah floor.

At the chain store Emily flicks through racks of tiny clothing. It will be Mahalia's first birthday soon and she is looking for a present.

'I feel okay about this,' she tells herself (she is often amazed at how okay she feels). But somehow she can't picture a real child, *her* child. It still seems so far away, somehow.

A woman walks down the aisle and stands beside her. She has a baby on her hip. The baby has wispy blonde hair and a high forehead. Emily glances at it and looks away.

'Will you just look at this little *dress?*' says the woman to no one in particular, so that Emily thinks that perhaps she must be talking to her. 'This is just so *cute!*'

'It is, isn't it?' mumbles Emily politely.

'Yes, I think this would suit you right down to the ground,' says the woman, and Emily realises with embarrassment that the woman has been talking to her baby, not to her.

Emily looks over at the baby, who stares back at her with a solemn expression on its face. She smiles at it, and the baby smiles back, looking bashful, tipping her head on one side and burrowing into her mother's shoulder.

'She's being a real little girl,' says the mother, and she really is speaking to Emily this time. 'It's that "Oh, don't look at me" thing.'

'How old is she?' asks Emily, shyly.

'Nine months,' says the woman with pride.

Emily reaches out and touches the baby's bare foot. It is plump and soft, with curled-up toes that wriggle around when Emily touches them. She is so *real*, so solid and actual. She has teeth, two at the top, and several at the bottom. She grinds her little teeth together and smiles at Emily again. She is such a patient, shy, cheerful baby.

'And . . . what's her name?'

'Emily.'

'Oh! That's . . . pretty.'

The woman has stopped looking at clothes and is smiling down at baby Emily. 'Isn't it?' she says with a smile. 'Well, best get on.' She takes the dress that she'd said would suit her baby right down to the ground and walks over to the checkout.

Emily feels tears running out of her eyes before she knows she is crying. She has no idea which dress would suit Mahalia. And she's never even seen her at the age that baby is – nine months. She's lost that, and can never get it back.

But she applies herself to examining the racks of clothes for one-year-olds. '*This* one,' she thinks, finding a little white frock with red polka dots all over the sleeves and around the hem.

When she gets back to Charlotte's that day she says, 'I think it's about time for me to go back.' She looks at Charlotte with alarm. It seems such a scary thing to do.

'Home,' she explains, when Charlotte looks puzzled.

Wherever that is.

2

But first, she wants to get her driver's licence.

And all the practice she's done pays off. She comes home late one afternoon with a provisional licence in her purse and P-plates on the car. She pulls up in the driveway and smiles at Charlotte. 'I'm going to ring my dad.'

'Great! I'll go out to the shed and leave you to it.'

Emily picks up the phone. Through the kitchen window she sees the light come on in Charlotte's shed. She takes the cordless receiver and sits with it on the back step. The twilight in the garden is pink and gold like some great frangipani and Charlotte's window at the back of the garden flames with light. Above the houses the sky is huge. With her knees pulled up to her chin Emily dials the number, hoping that her father will answer. He does.

'Hello . . . Dad?'

'Emmy! This is a nice surprise.'

Emily hurries on, surprised at how easy it is to talk to him. 'Dad, guess what – I got my licence today.'

'Oh, well done. First go?'

'Yes.'

'Good girl. I knew you would.'

'And I wanted to thank you for all the lessons you gave me, before . . .'

'Oh, that's all right . . .' He speaks awkwardly. He's never known what to say when he is thanked for something.

'Charlotte said that all she had to do was help me brush up a bit.'

'Yes, well . . . well done!' he says again. She hears him turning aside to speak to her mother. 'It's Emmy,' she hears him say. 'She has some news.'

Her mother comes on the line. 'Hello darling.'

'Hello Mum.' Emily unconsciously presses her fingernails into her knees as she speaks.

'What's your news?' asks her mother anxiously.

'Oh, it's just . . .' says Emily faintly, '. . . just that I got my P plates today.'

'Well! That is nice!' Her mother pauses. 'I thought you might be ringing to say that you were coming home.'

Emily pauses. 'Oh. Well, that too, I suppose.' The word *home* is a difficult one for her. 'I do want to come back soon,' she says, choosing her words carefully. 'Can I stay with you?'

'Of course,' says her mother, and adds awkwardly, 'after all, this is your home.'

After Emily has once more spoken to her father and promised to talk again soon, she puts the receiver down on the step beside her. She hugs her knees to her chest and stares out into the garden, watching the changing evening light. She looks at the silhouette of the leaves against the sky. Concentrating on things around her is a way of stopping herself from thinking. Then she allows herself to think about Matt, and Mahalia. She closes her eyes and remembers the scent of each of them: Matt after a day walking on the beach – salty and sharp, smelling of warmth and brown skin; Mahalia – new and clean, like fresh-cut grass.

3

The next morning, Emily goes out for a walk. It is unusual for her to be up quite so early, even now, but she feels invigorated after getting her licence. She walks past Martin's place. She has avoided it lately, expecting somehow never to see them again.

But she notices that the sneaker on the verandah has been tidied away. There is some sort of tree with small orange fruits sitting beside the door in a big pot. Down the side of the house, she sees a green tent airing on the clothesline.

The front door is open.

Emily is surprised by how her heart flips over. At least, she thinks it must be her heart, though it is more like a giant fish leaping in her belly. But she can't bring herself to walk up the veranda steps. She remembers the last time she saw Martin, and the last time she saw Cat, and Pete. Although the cut on her hand has healed, she remembers her shame.

But she is a different person, now.

'Can I borrow the car?' she asks Charlotte the next morning. It will be her first drive on her own.

'Of course,' says Charlotte. 'You may as well get some practice in. Are you planning on going far?'

'No – just to visit someone. Martin, actually, and Pete. I think they've come back from holiday.'

The sense of her own capability gives Emily pleasure as she sets off in the car on her own. She *is* a different person from the one who'd wandered the streets aimlessly, turning up on Martin's doorstep like a waif, but he won't know that. When she pulls up in front of their house she feels nervous.

The front door is shut. But even if it were open she'd knock. There is no sound from the house so she knocks a second time, and nervously adjusts the brim of her hat (the purple crocheted hat, the one they'd given her). She hears running footsteps, and the door is wrenched open by Pete, who stands looking at her with his mouth open. 'Emmy!' he says, and hugs her round the hips. He seems to have grown older. He has shot up, and seems less chubby and child-like. How can children change so fast?

'Did you have a great time at the beach?' she says.

'Sure did!' He walks down the hallway in front of her.

'Pete? Who is it?' Martin's voice comes from the bedroom.

'It's Emmy, Dad' says Pete, disappearing into the room. Emily follows him. Martin lies under the bedclothes, and gives her a weak smile.

'Dad's sick,' says Pete.

'Just a flu bug,' says Martin, closing his eyes.

'Can I do anything?'

'You could get me some water and a couple of Panadol.' Emily finds the medicine cupboard, and after he takes the tablets, Martin settles back and closes his eyes.

She finds a pile of dirty laundry next to the machine and puts it on to wash. While she waits for it to finish, she and Pete make sandwiches for lunch. She sends Pete to see if Martin is awake, but he's not.

After she hangs the washing out, Emily sits in the back yard and plays with Pete. She feels a great sense of satisfaction at the sheets flapping in the breeze. A sun skink runs across the path in front of the clothesline. *Who is here with us,* thinks Emily.

Pete has a pile of shells that he's collected at the beach, and they sort them into different kinds. He also has a dead seahorse that he found washed up. 'Poor seahorse,' says Emily, holding it up between her fingers to look closer. It has a salty, rather rotten smell, not unpleasant, and such a serious little face.

'Emmy,' says Pete, arranging shells into a pattern on the ground, 'do you ever think that you're dreaming everything?'

'I did think that once. But I think the world's real, now.'

She remembers Pete asking this question before.

'But what if it isn't? What if this is a dream?' Pete waves his arm around to encompass everything.

'Dreams are weirder than this,' says Emily. 'More . . . special.'

'But what if dreams are normal? What if in a dream you go to pre-school and make sandwiches, and in real life you can fly or something?'

'Well, you might have a point there, Pete. Maybe this is a dream.' Emily gets up and runs her hands over the sheets. She looks up at the blue sky, and as she moves away from the line sees only the fluttering of the white sheets. A black crow alights in the high branches of a tree next door and calls harshly. For a moment the world seems to slow down.

Then Pete calls, 'Emmy, watch this!' and before she can stop him he is running through the flapping sheets; blinded, he runs straight into the metal handle of the rotary clothes-line. She hears the crack of his head against the metal, his scream of pain, and then his face seems all blood. She rushes to kneel in front of him, pulling a towel from the line to staunch it.

There is a lot of blood gushing from the cut in his head. Emily attempts to soak it up, but fresh blood floods out. Pete is silent and pale. His breath comes in small gasps. 'How bad is it?' he asks.

'Not too bad,' says Emily, panicking inside. To her, it looks very bad. 'But I think you're going to need stitches.'

She gets him to hold the towel against his head, and picks him up and carries him into the house where she seats him at the kitchen table. She goes to Martin's room, but, amazingly, he is still asleep.

Emily makes a decision. She goes back to Pete and crouches in front of him. 'Look, I'm going to take you to the hospital. Okay?' Leaving a note for Martin on the table, she takes Pete out to the car.

At the hospital, after the nurse looks briefly at Pete's head, they wait for ages at reception. Finally Emily gets up and goes over to another nurse who has come on duty. 'How much longer is it going to be?' she asks. 'His head is still bleeding.'

'It could be a while,' says the woman sympathetically, coming over and looking at Pete but not bothering to examine his head. 'Head wounds do bleed a lot.'

'Look,' says Emily, 'I wonder if you could tell his mother? She works here, I think.' She looks questioningly at Pete, who nods.

'Her name is Cat . . .'

'Cat Hetherington?' prompts the nurse. 'Are you Pete?'

'Yes,' whispers Pete, looking very pale.

'I've heard about you!' she says warmly. 'Your mum won't be very happy to see you like this. I'll send her a message right now.'

She goes away, and soon they are taken to a room off a long corridor that appears to be a kind of storeroom. Pete lies on a high bed like a trolley, and Emily perches beside him, keeping the cloth pressed to his forehead. A nurse comes and takes his pulse. She explains that they have a lot of people in emergency and the doctor might be some time, and Emily must ring the buzzer if Pete starts vomiting or falling asleep.

After she has gone, Pete says, 'Emmy, I need to go to the toilet.'

She looks into the corridor, sees a toilet across the hallway, and helps him to it, keeping the towel pressed to his head. Back in the room where they have been put to wait, Pete lies on the bed without complaining, but she can see how anxious he is.

She casts around the room for distraction. 'I wonder what's in those boxes?' she asks, craning her neck to see what's stacked on top of the high cupboards. 'Tongue depressors,' she reads out, noting the illustration on the side. 'Like paddle-pop sticks, for when you open your mouth and say, "Ahh".'

'I know,' she says. 'Let's play I spy with my little eye. Have you ever played that?'

Pete sighs. 'Where's my mum?' he asks fretfully.

Another nurse arrives. She takes his pulse again and asks if he feels like vomiting at all. He doesn't, and that satisfies her; she goes away. Pete closes his eyes. His eyelids are patterned with delicate veins, and Emily feels a great surge of tenderness towards him, as if he were her own. 'Pete, you'd better not fall asleep on me, or they'll think you've fallen into a coma.'

'What's a coma?'

'It's when you pass out. Sort of go to sleep without being really asleep.'

'I think I know what you mean,' says Pete uncertainly. 'I won't.' After a while he says, 'Emmy?'

'Yes?'

'Do you think we're dreaming this?'

'I think it's real, Pete.'

'Me too.'

She takes his hand.

Someone comes in. It's Cat, looking very businesslike in a nurse's uniform.

'Mum!' says Pete. His face brightens, and he drops Emily's hand and sits up on one elbow to greet her.

'Pete. What on earth have you done?' She peels the towel away from Pete's forehead and examines it.

'Ran into the clothesline. Mum, where *were* you?'

'I was helping with an operation, so I've only just heard you were here.

'Where's Martin?' adds Cat, with an edge to her voice. She's looking across at Emily, who without thinking has moved away from Pete's side and is standing near the doorway, as though it might be handy if she needs to escape.

'He's sick,' says Emily. 'He was in bed asleep, so I left a note.'

'How on earth did you let this happen?'

'I couldn't stop it. He just ran into the clothesline. It was an accident.' Emily can feel herself speaking calmly and with dignity.

Cat doesn't comment. And at that moment the room seems filled with people. Two women have arrived, one with a stethoscope slung round her neck, the other wheeling a trolley, and Emily feels she's in the way, so she takes the opportunity to slip out the door.

Once she'd have removed herself from the scene, but now she stands outside in the corridor, leaning against the wall. She can feel it against the back of her head. She looks up at fluorescent lights lining the ceiling, and down at grey vinyl tiles on the floor. She waits.

When it seems she has been there an eternity, Cat emerges from the room. She hesitates, and then takes up a position facing Emily against the opposite wall. 'I didn't think you'd still be here.'

Emily asks, 'How is he?'

'He'll be okay. They're taping up the cut.'

Emily closes her eyes. She'd worried that it might have been worse. 'That's good,' she says.

'I just need to know,' says Cat, 'exactly how it happened.'

Her face, under the harsh lights, looks crumpled and exhausted.

Emily swallows. 'Martin was ill and he fell asleep. I did a

load of washing. And while we were out in the yard waiting for it to dry, Pete ran through one of the sheets and cracked his head on the pole. He must have hit some sharp part of the handle or something.'

She looks up at the ceiling again and relives it all happening, in slow motion.

'It happened before I could do a thing.'

They both turn their heads as a figure appears at the end of the corridor. Together they watch Martin hurry towards them. Tall, dishevelled, feverish-looking, he hesitates as he comes close. 'How's Pete?' His voice is urgent.

'The doctor's in there with him – he'll be fine. A scar, probably. That's all he'll have, a bit of a scar.' But Cat sounds bitter.

Martin leans against the wall. The three of them stand silently in awkward geometry, Martin and Cat on one side of the narrow corridor, and Emily on the other. A man in a white coat goes past and says quietly, 'Excuse me, please,' as though he's interrupting something.

'I got your note,' says Martin, to Emily. 'How did it happen?'

'I'll tell you later,' Cat breaks in irritably. 'I don't want to have to listen to it again.'

'Anyway, how did you get him here?' Martin persists. Just woken from sleep, he seems to be still trying to grasp the situation.

'I drove.'

'Drove! You *drove* him yourself?' Cat is incredulous.

'I have my licence,' says Emily. She is suddenly tired of all this. She looks across at Martin. 'I think I may as well go.'

Cat glances at her, then looks at Martin. 'We can take Pete home once they're finished in there. I'm almost at the end of my shift anyway.' She wipes her hand wearily across her face. 'I've been staring at blood all day.'

'Can we go and see him?'

As Cat directs Martin into the room, he turns distractedly and waves, 'Thanks, Emily.'

She treads down the brilliantly lit corridor, and then out through the waiting room. At the entrance to the Casualty Department she pauses to remember where she parked the car. She feels in her pocket for the keys.

Emily walks to the lookout and watches the transformation of day into night. There is no suddenness to it, just an impercep-tible change in the colour of the sky, and the slow appearance of stars, like something welling up from the depths of water. With the dark comes a welcome coolness. It is now the middle of summer.

She begins to walk back, and finds herself in Martin's street (her feet perhaps remembering the way), and then she is in front of his house. She is leaving tomorrow and has left it too late to say goodbye.

The front door is shut. But as she watches, Martin happens to let himself out and walks down the path.

'Emily?'

'Hi,' she says shyly, hands in the pockets of her new cotton jeans.

'You were about to visit?' He nods towards his house.

'Well, thinking of it. But it's Pete's bedtime, isn't it?'

They begin to walk. Emily has not seen Martin for days – not since she took Pete to the hospital.

'How's Pete's head?'

'Recovering. And I'm much better, too. Since you asked.'

He grins at her, and in reply she grins back, and begins to run.

She hears his footsteps pounding behind her, and quickens her flight. She has no idea why she is running, but keeps going, enjoying the rush of her blood, the feeling it gives her of being alive, a sense of danger and light and possibility that she's not felt in a long time.

It's an exhilarating headlong dash along the darkened paths, lit by occasional streetlamps. She feels sure and swift on her feet, completely in control of her movements. Her head is clear. She stops at intersections, panting, waiting for cars to pass, and then propels herself forward again.

Suddenly she stops and turns, pivoting. She sees him behind her, slowing to a slow-motion stride as he approaches.

She has the urge to dash away again and stands poised. Martin holds his arms out as though to embrace her, but as he comes up to her he swings them down to his sides.

Emily relaxes and stands squarely on her two feet.

'I'm leaving tomorrow,' she says. 'Going home.'

They start to walk.

'Back to your baby? Mahalia.' He says the name tenderly.

She glances up at him.

'You're different,' he says.

She nods with satisfaction. 'Better,' she says. 'You've no idea how good it is.'

The lights are on in most of the houses. Emily likes the warmth they promise, each light a little beacon of life. They come to a church, not the Catholic one, and pause to gaze at the reflection of a small tree next to a pool of water out the front. The leaves shiver, showing their silvery undersides. Emily dips her hand into the water, splintering the image. She places drops of water onto her forehead; when they run down to her mouth she licks them away.

A man and a woman run up the stone steps at the side of the building, arm in arm, laughing, breathless, clutching large sheafs of paper. One of them fumbles with a key, and they let themselves in. Moments later the sound of organ music comes out, faltering at first, then joyous.

In the park, they are the only ones there. They take a swing each and, while Martin drifts lazily to and fro, Emily pushes herself higher and higher until she feels she is almost flying. When she's had enough she slows the swing down, and when it's almost at a standstill, jumps off and says, 'Tomorrow's a big day for me – I need to get some sleep. Can you say goodbye to Pete for me?'

'I'll walk you home.'

Outside Charlotte's place, Emily looks at him in sudden panic.

'What if my baby doesn't *like* me? What if we don't *bond*?'

He simply looks at her, kindly.

'I know,' she says. 'It'll be okay in the end.'

She lets herself in the front door while he stands and watches. She doesn't close the door straight away, but waits for him to move away down the street, out of the pool of light.

Five

I

When the boarding call is announced, Emily gets to her feet at once and kisses Charlotte; she doesn't want to appear ungrateful, but it seems useless to linger. She is the first to be ushered down the steps and into the bus that is to take them to the plane. The other passengers stroll on, some of them greeting business colleagues. The bus starts up, and she is swayed this way and that as it pulls out and makes its way to the small plane, which sits on the runway, dwarfed by larger aircraft. She disembarks and goes up the narrow springy steps to a beaming steward. She finds her seat and stows her bag. Everything seems to take so *long*.

She watches the safety instructions anxiously. Take-off is a long breathless battle of wills as the plane fights gravity to become airborne, and she only exhales and settles back when it levels out.

Sydney lies beneath them, red brick suburbs and cliffs and blue, white-capped waves. And then they leave it behind. She peers from the window, sometimes onto a fantasy landscape of fluffy white cloud, and sometimes at forests and the geometry of farmland and rivers. Emily is intent on noticing everything. If she pays attention to *things* she won't have to think of *her*, imagine *her*.

The sea below is the one constant, the mantra she keeps returning to. When she sees the town of Coffs Harbour, tears spring to her eyes. They are now very close to home.

They fly inland again, and soon, instead of looking at anonymous landscape, Emily begins to recognise places that she knows. They are asked to fasten their seat belts as they begin their descent.

Lismore tilts beneath them as the plane banks. She sees the golf club where her father plays, and the tip, and the council swimming pool. And now she permits herself to imagine.

Somewhere down there is her baby.

The plane wheels above the town in a kind of salute and then rushes onto the runway, drawing up with a shudder like a huge plunging horse suddenly come to its senses.

She barely hears the smooth voice of the pilot thanking them for flying and telling them cosily that the temperature in Lismore is a very warm thirty-one degrees. She is peering from the window at the glass-fronted terminal, and she sees her father standing there at the front, with his hand up to shade his eyes from the late afternoon sun.

She walks up to him shyly and kisses his cheek. He puts his arms around her awkwardly at first, and she allows herself to cling.

'Your mum stayed home to watch the dinner,' he says, and she's pleased to have a few minutes' respite. Her father has brought out his old car for a run; as she slips into the seat she smells the familiar cracked varnish and old leather.

His hair looks thinner; he's brushed it over the top to conceal the bare patch, and it looks oddly touching to Emily. She thinks, with a pang of dismay, *But he's old!*

'Do you reckon you can remember how to drive this one?' he asks teasingly, and she replies, with a grin, 'With a bit of practice. You'll have to give me a few lessons.'

'Good girl,' he says, the way he always spoke to Grandad's horses. She smiles at him again, and they hold each other's eyes for a moment.

The house smells of roast meat. Her father carries her bag down the hall to her old room, and Emily walks through to the kitchen. Her mother straightens up from checking the oven and turns awkwardly to her. She folds a teatowel carefully and places it on the table. Is it possible that she's feeling nervous too?

Emily goes forward. 'Mum . . .'

'Emily . . .'

They hold each other in the barest of embraces, and her mother's hands flutter out beside her afterwards, not knowing what to do next. She turns to the saucepans on the stove. 'Did you have a good flight?'

'Yes . . . it seemed to take no time at all.'

'Charlotte just rang to say she'd only just got back to the mountains – ridiculous, isn't it?'

They prattle nervously as her mother busies herself with cooking. Emily stares at her mother's back and it seems to her to be both apologetic and stubborn, which is basically how Emily herself is feeling. Will they ever be able to exist together happily?

Finally her mother says, 'Dinner won't be long. Would you like a shower first? – you must be feeling sticky from the trip,' and Emily is released, to go to her room, to finger all her forgotten things – her childish collection of little ponies, the duck pencil-sharpeners, the porcelain statue of a brown horse – and to notice how dreadfully pink everything is (the bedspread, the walls, the furniture) – so pink that the late afternoon sun coming through the window fairly blazes with it.

On the way to the shower she spies something through the doorway of the spare room. It is a white wooden cot, all made up with white sheets and pillowcases with bears embroidered on them. She lifts up the pillow and smells it, and it has the clean scent of something washed and dried in the sunshine, with another scent underlying it. It is the scent of her baby.

2

She is here, in the same town, and Emily can't wait to see her. But she can't just yet – and it seems absurd to have to wait, but Matt doesn't even know she's coming, and anyway, it's getting late. *Only one more sleep* . . . she tells herself, but her feeling is more urgent than that. She's here, in the same town, but her baby still seems too far away.

'Can I borrow your car in the morning?' she asks her mother at dinner. The sound of their knives and forks scraping against the plates seems deafening.

'Oh – I'll drive you down,' says her mother, laying down a fork full of roast potato.

'It's all right, I have my licence now,' says Emily. 'If you don't mind,' she adds firmly, 'I'd rather go on my own.'

That night she lies with the window above her bed open and the curtains pulled back to catch the breeze. She doesn't sleep much at all, just lies staring through the window at the sky. But she doesn't cry, or even feel remotely like it.

It seems the longest drive she's ever taken in her life, yet it's only a few kilometres. Once she gets to the roundabout at the top of the hill it's just one long swoop down the hill to the city centre.

The place is in a broad old street of timber houses – an old two-storeyed shop (her mother has described it to her and she remembers passing it on the way home from school sometimes) with the front windows painted over and a peeling front door.

She parks a little way down the street and sits quietly for a moment, with her eyes closed and her head against the steering wheel. No thought will stay focussed for more than a moment. And then she gets out of the car, locking the door and walking quickly away down the street.

It's still quite early – just after nine – and there are numerous cars making their way into town, which lies just across a wooden bridge. She walks up to the bridge and over it, looking down at the water. She goes back, passing an old red-brick pub on the corner overlooking the river, then several shops, and a couple of decrepit timber cottages. She imagines Matt and Mahalia walking up and down this road every day. This is their place, this has been their life, and she's not had any part in it for what feels like a very long time.

Emily goes past the building where they live three times before she gets up the courage to knock, her heart pounding. She hears footsteps, and then Matt is standing there looking exactly as she remembered him, and for a moment it seems all right – almost.

Later, she can't even remember the first thing she said, but thinks it must have been something dumb and obvious. She remembers stepping forward and putting her arms around him briefly, the pang of the scent of him, the awkwardness of his body. She remembers him showing her down a dark hallway. Halfway down she turned back and smiled at him, and encountered such a look of sorrow that her heart flipped over with dismay. But she can't begin to think how to deal with Matt; it is enough to be thinking about Mahalia. They come to a bright shabby kitchen, and a door leading out the back. She hears a child talking cheerfully to herself in baby talk.

3

And then there she is. Your baby. She is playing in a sandpit in the small back yard, and when you arrive she turns, waving a plastic spade and immediately plopping down onto her bottom. 'Da?' she says, her face lighting up, and it's not you she's smiling at, but Matt.

You crouch in front of her. *And it's not your baby, after all.* This one is so big – and her face is all wrong; it's not the same shape. And her hair is so long it's already been cut – she has a proper fringe, and blunt bits at the back where it's been trimmed. You turn to Matt – surely something has happened to the baby you had together, and he's found another one to replace her. But no, he's picking her up, and talking to her softly, saying something about *your mum*. And the baby – Mahalia – *your* baby – snuggles into his shoulder and then peeks out at you shyly. And now you can see that it *is* her – she hasn't changed so much really. And you reach out and take her hand, or as much of her hand as she will allow, which is just the tip of a little finger.

4

The first time Emily takes her out on her own, Mahalia screams and screams. Emily has been visiting her every day for a week, and Mahalia has been happy enough to play on the swings and let Emily feed her lunch, opening her mouth obediently and then taking hold of the spoon to feed herself. Now she screams and wriggles on the bed while Emily tries to change her nappy. *She hates me,* Emily thinks in panic, *and no wonder . . .* But then a voice that might be Martin's comes to her, and it says, reasonably, *All babies get like that sometimes. Anyway, she'll get used to you, just give it time.*

So she picks her up and talks softly through the complaints, walking round the bedroom and giving her a bright pink toy horse to hold. 'Hor,' says Mahalia, the tears stopping as quickly as they started, staring at the toy with a look of stunned amazement.

'Do you want a swim in the pool?' says Emily, and the baby looks at her questioningly. She lies her down on the bed to undress her. The baby kicks her foot against her in a slow, testing movement, and Emily grasps it and holds it gently. Mahalia looks at Emily with interest. Emily smiles. Mahalia pushes her foot against Emily's hand and, enjoying the resistance, does it again.

Emily puts her nose against the baby's belly and breathes in the smell of her.

She undresses Mahalia and then takes off her own clothes, and carries her through the house and out to her parents' pool, where she lifts the latch on the child-proof gate and goes in.

Going into the water, she can feel Mahalia clinging to her hips with her knees, and one small hand holding on to her hair, the other to her breast. A strong, sweet feeling of love and possessiveness overtakes her, and she kisses her baby so hard that they both gasp.

She hadn't counted on this – on her own greed. She loves Mahalia so much that she wants her all to herself.

One day, as she picks her up from Matt's place she says, 'Look, Matt, I should tell you something. I'd like Mahalia to come and live with me.'

In the face of his dismay, she hesitates and says, 'Think about it, yeah?'

The next time she comes to pick up Mahalia, they have gone.

One of the girls who shares the house with Matt opens the door. 'I'm sorry,' she says (and she does look sorry), 'but they're not here.'

'Do you know when they'll be back?'

'No. I meant, they've gone away for a while. I don't know where. Matt left a note.'

'Can I go up to their room?'

'Sure.'

Emily takes herself up the dark stairway to their room at the front of the building. The yellow room, which is a grimy, dull yellow, not a happy colour at all, feels abandoned. Mahalia's cot is folded up against the wall, and a few of her clothes are scattered over the floor. Emily kneels down and unconsciously puts her nose to a tiny shirt, and her throat closes up. It looks to her as though they've gone for good.

A fly buzzes against the glass of the verandah door. Emily opens it, releasing the insect, and steps out. There is a yellowing newspaper on the floor out there. A clothesline strung across the space holds several faded plastic pegs. She goes to the railing and looks down into the street. A girl on a bicycle rides past, glancing up and waving as though she knows the occupants. A black dog noses in the gutter. Emily finds some old wind chimes lying in a corner of the verandah; she picks them up and they clack with a soft, harsh sound. She throws them down again and they lie there like bones.

She looks around and takes a breath. This is where Mahalia has lived for most of the time she's been away. All the time Emily was in the mountains, wandering the windy streets, sleeping in Pete's bed in the afternoons and having cups of tea with Martin in the garden, this has been her life. Emily has been unable to imagine it. She was afraid to imagine it, but now she is here and they are gone she feels pain and sweet nostalgia.

Downstairs, the front room is a mess of boxes and old

furniture; it looks as though it's used as a storeroom. There's a sound from the kitchen, and Emily walks down the short hallway in that direction. The girl who'd opened the door (Eliza, is it? Emily can barely remember her name) stands at the opened refrigerator eating fruit yoghurt from a large tub. She's dressed in a fancy, old white lace petticoat, and scuffed work boots.

'I'm going now,' says Emily. 'Can you let them know I was looking for them?'

The girl licks yoghurt from her lips and puts the tub away. She has a head of long curls that she has to keep flinging back from her face. 'I'll see you out,' she says, and follows Emily back down the hall. Emily can hear the sound of her boots tramping behind her; she's very heavy on her feet.

Emily returns to her parents' place.

'Where's Mahalia?' says her mother.

'They weren't there.'

Emily speaks without evident emotion, but inside she has a spring coiled up, threatening to unwind. If she allows it to snap she will let out a long, agonising wail.

She goes and lies on her bed. She won't allow herself to cry. In a little while she gets up and rings Matt's mother, who says that they aren't at her place without a hint in her voice that something might be wrong.

So perhaps it's nothing. They've just gone away for a day or two.

She paces about the house, can't eat, and finally lies sleepless in the dark. Her father comes and sits on the edge of the bed, smoothing the hair from her forehead. 'We'll figure something out,' he says. 'She'll be okay. Try to get some sleep.'

Very much later, as she still lies there with dry eyes, her mother appears at the doorway, a silhouette against the night-light in the hall. 'Emily?' she says, in a hesitant voice. 'May I come in?'

Emily doesn't reply, but she feels the mattress dip as her mother sits down next to her. It creaks as Emily turns round to face her; her mother is a padded shape in the dark, round and plump in a summer brunch coat. She never wears perfume, but ever since Emily can remember she has smelt of the same floral bath soap. She doesn't say anything, but reaches out and takes Emily's hand. Emily can hear her clock ticking, her pink ballerina clock that she's had since she was a child. The numerals on its face are lit up in the darkness. It must have been steadily ticking away like that all the time she's been away.

Emily knows that she doesn't need to do or say anything, simply sit there with her mother's hand in hers. She falls asleep with her mother sitting there beside her. When she wakes in the morning it has come to her where Matt and Mahalia might be.

6

It isn't possible to drive all the way to the van. There is a parking place near the top of the hill; from there on you have to go on foot. It is mid-morning, shrill with cicadas, by the time Emily walks into the clearing where Matt watches her approach. Mahalia is nowhere to be seen.

She is in the van, exclaiming over a butterfly flapping against the glass. Matt opens the window and lets it go, and Mahalia cries. Matt picks her up and sings to her to quiet her.

'You've learned to sing,' says Emily, her words seeming to rasp, sounding strange to herself. Emily looks at her baby with surprise. She still isn't used to the *realness* of her.

'You funny little thing,' she says with wonder.

She bends down to look into Mahalia's face and says firmly, in a louder voice, 'You're a funny little thing. Do you know that?'

Emily takes Mahalia down to the bed, which is unmade and tangled with limp bedclothes. She lies down and closes her eyes. Her body remembers being here. She imagines she can still smell herself on the sheets. Her fingers reach back onto a shelf above the bed and find a pair of star-shaped earrings; she tucks them into the pocket of her jeans.

She remembers how it had been then. But this is now.

She can feel the sweet weight of Mahalia clambering on top of her and makes no effort to push her away. Everything seems like a dream; she is sick and light-headed from grief and lack of sleep. And she finds herself somehow at the door of the van, and then outside, staring out at the hills, at that view, which once enthralled and then oppressed her.

'I was too young. We were both too young. We should never have had her.'

And it feels like the truth and not the truth at the same time, but someone has said it. It must have been her, because Matt is crying. Real, unfettered tears are coming from his eyes, falling like rain. 'Don't *say* that. Don't *say* that!'

'I'm sorry. I'm really sorry.'

She knows that it isn't all right to wish that your own child had never been born. She thinks fiercely that even though she now loves Mahalia enough to kill for her, enough to hurt Matt beyond belief it seems, it is still the way she feels.

'There's no chance of us getting together again, is there.' It isn't a question that he's asking.

'No,' she says. 'It's gone beyond that.'

She can hear herself swallow.

Matt says, 'You should have seen her the first time she walked. I might easily have missed it, but I was there.

'She was holding herself up with this bloody washing basket and pushing it along. And then she saw me and let go . . .'

He has tears in his eyes. She can see he's almost crying. But he blinks them away.

She and Matt spend a long time talking. Emily has an impression of hours passing, though it's probably only minutes.

162

By the time they've finally packed up and left the van for good, it is still not much after midday.

Matt says, the words coming from him with difficulty, 'I just want you to explain why you went away.'

Emily looks out at the endless view – all that blue sky. Despite the difficulties she and Matt are having now, a feeling of hope and possibility has returned to her. She isn't the same person who had gone away. She isn't even the same person that Matt had once known, when they had planned for their baby with such foolish confidence.

No ordinary words can explain how she had felt. The heaviness, and blackness. The feeling of having a weight inside her, but at the same time having a huge hole there, too.

So Emily tries, and stumbles; she can hear how feeble it sounds, because no words can convey that feeling. So she rushes in with more words, and that's all they are: words to fill in the spaces, because no one could understand. She doesn't even understand it herself, and now that it's over it seems as though it has all happened long ago, or in a dream, or to someone else.

She sees Mahalia, sitting on the ground putting stones into an old plastic pot, with such intent and beautiful concentration. Emily feels with exultation, *I love her. I love her!* She runs over and squats in front of her and tickles her on her fat foot. Mahalia squirms and laughs. 'Incy-wincy spider,' says Emily, walking her fingers up Mahalia's leg.

But then Matt comes over and seizes the baby, scooping her up from the ground and holding her so tightly Emily thinks that he might crush her. She goes to him and puts her hand to his cheek. Her fingers are pale against his brown skin. 'Don't *look* like that,' she says.

'Like what?'

Like you want to die, or something. Emily doesn't say anything.

Mahalia wriggles to get free and he puts her on the ground.

'I'm *good* at looking after her,' he says. 'It's what I do *really well*. I won't let you take her away from me!'

Then Emily says the thing she almost instantly regrets, and the words seem to make the world stop. Even the cicadas cease their shrilling. Only Mahalia continues doing what she is doing, contentedly and steadily putting stones into the pot. And when she's filled it up at last she tips them all out onto the ground again.

Afterwards, Emily drops Matt and Mahalia back at *their place*, and it feels like that, their place, as she watches them go up to the old shop door, where Matt puts their belongings down on the ground and searches in his pockets for the key. Emily doesn't wait for them to go in. In the rear-view mirror she sees Mahalia still waving to her as she drives away.

Emily doesn't go back to her parents straight away. She stops the car down near the river to think, and sits with the afternoon sun blazing in. She doesn't like to think of what she said to Matt up at the van, but she has to remember it and own up to it.

She said, 'I could take it court!'

And at that moment she meant it, because she wanted Mahalia all to herself.

'And you'd probably win,' said Matt, sounding defeated. 'Because you're her mother ... But you don't want that, do you?'

'No,' she admitted defensively.

It won't come to that. Some people would say that Matt had won. But there isn't any winning where children are concerned, and maybe Mahalia has won, because they've agreed, after all that, to share looking after her.

'Let her keep living with me,' Matt said. 'For now, anyway. I don't want to take her away from you – I'd never do that. But she's her own person. Getting more like that every day. Maybe one day she'll want to go and live with you.'

Emily thinks about the old shop that has been Mahalia's home since she's been away; the room painted dirty yellow, the verandah with the weathered timber floor, and people who cycle past and wave. The back yard has a sandpit. It isn't a bad place for a baby. And Matt looks after her well, she can see that.

Emily starts the car and points the nose homewards.

7

(A postcard: the north head of the Brunswick River and New Brighton beach from the air)

Dear Pete,

This is the beach where I am today. There are some rocks in the water in front of me that look like a whole lot of shark fins, and I've just met a dog that wants me to keep throwing a stick for it to fetch. It's a cute dog, so ugly it's almost beautiful. It was great to get your phone call. I forgot that you were starting school this year — is it still good fun? I am also at school now, and Martin's probably told you I have a baby, called Mahalia — maybe you'll meet her one day.

Lots of luv,

Emmy XXXX

Dear Martin,

It was amazing to get a call from you and Pete last week — of course I hadn't forgotten you. But I'm terrible at keeping in contact with people.

Fancy you being back teaching this year! But with Pete at school I guess you don't need to stay home. I'm back at school, too. It's okay too — just! — but difficult with a baby. Sometimes I get so tired I want to scream. I'm really lucky that Matt and I share looking after her, and my parents are keen babysitters, so is Matt's mother — so as you can see I have it pretty easy really.

I didn't say a lot on the phone the other night because my parents were kind of hanging around. So what am I doing? — can't even remember what I told you cos I was so excited to hear from you — I'm living at home with my parents. That's okay — we're all trying to get along, which we do mostly.

Matt and I didn't get together again but we have kind of figured things out — for now. We share looking after Mahalia, but she's with Matt most of the time.

I have plans for the future. At the moment I'm living at home till I finish my HSC, which will be the end of next year. Then I want to get into uni here at Lismore. I had all sorts of wild ideas at first of going away and studying to be a vet or something glamorous, but with Matt living here I have to stick around. And — can you believe this? — I have almost decided that I will do primary teaching. So many reasons — like getting the school hols off etc., but I also think I'm pretty good at being with little kids — and I like them. When I do go to uni I'd like to get a flat on my own or go into a share house or something.

AND . . . I'm hoping to bring Mahalia to the Blue Mountains after Christmas for a holiday to see Charlotte, and visit you all. She'll be almost two then — should I start getting worried? I can sometimes see my mother looking at us both when Mahalia's playing up a bit and thinking, Just you wait till she's a teenager!

That's all for now. I'm on my own here today. Sometimes I bring Mahalia, but she's with Matt this weekend. He and I plan to bring her to the beach together in a couple of weeks. As you can see from my card to Pete, this beach is long and almost deserted. There are a few houses along the beachfront, but you can't see them from the beach — it's all bush.

Who is here with me: a black dog that wants me to throw a stick for it (for the umpteenth time); two seagulls squabbling over a piece of old fish; a pregnant woman in a bikini holding the hand of her toddler in the surf; someone doing yoga; a small sand crab.

Please write back!

Love,

Emily
XXX

Emily folds the letter and puts it into her bag. It seems such a long letter but it still hasn't told Martin everything. There are some things that she thinks you can never tell other people. *Do you know what I think?* she could have written. *I think that people are mysterious and unknowable, especially your own self. I'm still finding out things about myself that I'd never dreamed possible.*

Pulling off her T-shirt and hat, she runs down to the water and makes her way out into the waves, broaching them side-on until finally she takes a deep breath and dives under.

She stays in the surf till she's waterlogged, emerges exhilarated, and flops down at the place where the waves run up onto the sand, the magical place where the sea kisses the land, and where the damp sand reflects the sky, so that it appears almost luminous.

She spreads herself out in a star shape and closes her eyes, rolling back and forth on her back in the shallow water. The only thing she can hear is the pounding of the waves – or

168

perhaps it's her own heartbeat. After a while she opens her eyes and looks at the sky.

She had forgotten that it's such a clear, transparent blue.

(A postcard: *Paris through the Window, by Marc Chagall, 1913*)

The frame of the window is streaked with bright colours, yellow, red, green and blue. A bunch of flowers sits on a chair beneath it. A yellow cat with a human face sits on the sill. There is a figure in the right bottom corner with two heads, one of them blue. The city is outlined, with the Eiffel Tower predominating. The tiny figures of a man and a woman lie outstretched, floating. They look like insects. A man floats suspended in the sky beneath a triangular shape that could be a parachute.

It is such a mad, joyful, colourful picture that looking at it makes Emily smile.

She turns the postcard over and reads it again.

Hi Emily,

Took my Year Six class down to the city to the Art Gallery and found this card in the shop. Thought of you the moment I saw it – isn't it great? No angels this time, just ordinary (ordinary?) people.

Looking forward to you bringing Mahalia to the mountains in the holidays. Pete's wondering if she'll be able to play soccer – it's his latest thing.

Letter following (when I find the time) – or I'll phone if I'm lazy.

Cat says to say Hi.

Love,

Martin

Emily slides the postcard into the textbook she's meant to be reading. 'Mahalia!' she calls. 'Put your hat back on!'

Matt says, 'She's always hated hats,' and runs over to where she's thrown it down. He goes after her and pops it back onto her head, tying it again under her chin. A woman walking past smiles at them all; Emily can see that she thinks they're a family – which they are, after a fashion.

Emily lies down and soaks up the late winter sun. She has a lightness that is new to her. At the same time she is heavy, but a pleasant heaviness, grounded in the earth. She feels a new pleasure in her body. Rubbing sunscreen into her belly she notices the faintest of marks there, a few fine, silvery lines where the skin had pulled and stretched when she was pregnant. On her inner arms the scars have also faded and are almost unnoticeable. Matt certainly doesn't seem to have noticed them, though she doesn't go out of her way to display that part of her body. *I have changed*, she thinks. *I've lived. I've made mistakes and I've survived.*

In the mountains it will still be cold and misty and damp.

She thinks of Martin in his heavy black coat – how he seemed to recognise her that day at the lookout. 'I didn't see you standing there,' he'd said. It astonishes her that it was a whole year ago she was there.

She looks over at Matt; he is sitting upright on his towel; never once has he taken his eyes from Mahalia. They both watch as she struggles up the soft sand towards them, spilling water from her bucket; she sings, over and over, in three descending notes, 'La, la, la . . . La, la, la . . .'

'Who's been teaching her to sing?' says Emily. 'Eliza?'

Matt blushes and grins. 'Yeah.'

'Don't be embarrassed,' says Emily teasingly. 'I know you two are an item. I'm okay with that.'

Though she wonders whether she is, really.

Emily looks at the sea where the waves roll in, the foam on their crests like the manes of galloping horses. 'Remember the time I rode that horse up the beach?' she says.

Matt grins and looks at her shyly.

'I was so . . .'

'What?'

'Carefree. Self-centred. Still am a bit. I'm the most im-perfect person I know.'

She looks at him. 'It was difficult, wasn't it? While I was away. Looking after Mahalia on your own.'

He doesn't reply for a while, and then says, 'It was what I had to do. What I wanted to do.'

Emily lets sand slip through her fingers. 'You know,' she says, 'I really did love you. And I feel . . . so *sad* sometimes about all that.' For a moment she thinks she's going to cry.

'Come for a walk,' he says, and pulls her to her feet.

And they fetch Mahalia from where she is digging and walk up the beach towards the mouth of the river. Emily carries Mahalia on her hip, where she sits holding on to Emily's shirt with one hand, while waving the other hand in the air. She's like an appendage – an extra limb, say, or a little wing, flapping joyfully as they make their way up the beach.

'Do you know what I'd like?' Emily tells Matt, after they've stopped so Mahalia can pat an old golden retriever. 'I'd like us not to be too fearful for her. Not cocoon her too much. Let her play with dogs and run about outside and make cubbies and things. I'd like to bring her up not to be afraid. To learn how to make mistakes and recover from them. The world's not that dangerous, right?'

Matt nods and grins, slinging Mahalia up onto his hip.

All the way up the beach they pass her back and forth between them, and when they come to the breakwater they climb up to look at where the river enters the sea. They search for the whales that can often be seen quite close to the shore, but there are none. And when they've had enough looking, they make their way down to the sand again. Matt goes first, clambering down over the rocks. At the bottom he looks up expectantly and holds out his arms.

'Are you ready, Mahalia? One, two, three . . .' Emily swings Mahalia out over the rocks, and Matt receives her and holds her close.